Chili to Die For

A Willow Crier Cozy Mystery

Lilly York

Chili to Die For

A Willow Crier Cozy Mystery

Book 1

Cover Design: Jonna Feavel
40daygraphics.com

Illustrations: Ben Gerhards

Interior Layout: Daniel Mawhinney
40daypublishing.com

Published by: Wide Awake Books
wideawakebooks.com

Also available in eBook publication

The following is a work of fiction. Names, characters, places, and incidents are fictitious or used fictitiously. Any resemblance to real persons, living or dead, to factual events or to businesses is coincidental and unintentional.

Printed in the United States of America

Get your free short story!

Grandpa Goes Missing

Find out what happened to bring Willow down to Oklahoma in the first place.

FREE short story only available here!

www.lillyyork.com/shortstory

Get yours today!

Chapter 1

"What did I do?" Willow mostly asked herself as she watched the woman's mouth going a mile a minute as the car pulled alongside her own. She couldn't hear a thing, of course both sets of windows were up. She tilted her head and tried to read her lips. Nope. She was still clueless.

The woman pulled around Willow and into the turn lane. Hands flying as she drove the big old white Cadillac. She'd had enough. Willow stopped her late model Cherokee right next to the monstrous tank and rolled down her window. Now it was Willow's turn. She was tired of reading lips.

"What did I do?" She said again.

The woman yelled across her passenger seat and out the window. "It's 50 through here."

"And?"

"You were going 30."

"And?"

"If you can't go the speed limit then get your…"

Willow cut her off before she could go any further. "For your information, 50 is the maximum speed allowed. Not really sure if you know how that works, but I don't have to go 50. I can go 30 if I want to." She knew she irritated these Southern drivers, but old habits were hard to break. There were days she missed her northern dwelling place and this was one of them. Get caught doing 50 in town up there and you'd find yourself with a hefty ticket. "Have you ever heard of passing? There are two lanes here, ya know?"

"Passing? I'll give you passing."

Willow raised her eyebrows as the woman reached across her ample lap to undo her seat belt. *Okay, here we go.* She raised her window and waited for the drama to start. The woman was standing outside her window within a few seconds. Willow readied her phone and started snapping pictures. In one, the woman looked as if she was rabid. She was so mad spittle was leaking out the corners of her mouth. Willow took a picture just as she put her hands on the window, opened her mouth, and went crazy-eyed. That would make an awesome road rage post. Willow noticed other people standing outside their cars taking videos on their phones. This was going to light up Facebook, she was sure of it. Cars started honking when the light turned green. She just laughed, stuck out her tongue, put her Jeep in gear, and waved goodbye.

"Really, Willow? That is the best you could come up with?" The commotion caused her to miss her turn. She shook her head and patted the bag of ingredients sitting in the truck next to her. "It's okay. We'll be home before you know it. A little detour won't hurt." 30 minutes later, Willow pulled off a country road onto her long dirt driveway in the little town of Turtle, Oklahoma. She looked around at the property. This was why she moved to Oklahoma. This was why she left the comfort of her childhood home and moved to a foreign land. She loved it and she hated it. But, mostly, she loved it.

After carrying in her groceries, she tried to turn on the stove top to heat up her pot. *Nothing.* Willow hit the element with her spatula and waited to see the familiar red. Still nothing. *Ugh.*

She knew this day was coming.

Willow pulled down a microwave safe bowl and started heating up small batches of ground beef. *This is going to be a long night.*

Chapter 2

Willow carefully carried her pot of chili into the contest entry area in the cafeteria of the high school gym. This was her second competition and she was so excited. Even though her stove decided to break at the most inopportune time, her chili was going to knock em' dead. It was probably the best chili she'd ever made. She had a bowl for lunch just to make sure it was edible. Like she had any doubts. Her mouth would be on fire for the rest of the day. She didn't care. It was that good.

She set her pot down at the entry table and checked in. She had registered several weeks before and had sent in a copy of her recipe. She was given a contestant badge and a name tag. Molly, the event hostess, led her to her station.

"You've got a chafing dish and sterno to reheat your chili. I've run across you at a few of these now. Do you enter them often?"

Molly had a strong Southern accent. Willow took a moment to decipher her words. "This is my second time. I won second place in the stew competition last month. I have to admit, I'm hooked." She smiled.

Molly raised her eyebrows. "You do know this here contest is for amateurs only, right? You aren't a trained chef or somethin', are ya?"

"Oh, no. I just love to putter around in the kitchen and try out new recipes. I did inherit a little ice cream shop. I wouldn't call that being a professional chef though. I just serve ice cream and sweet treats." She looked alarmed. "Does that count as being a professional?"

Molly laughed. "No, I reckon you're safe then."

"Oh, good. I do some of the baking in house and a lady in town, Mrs. Cookie Crumble, provides me with fresh made cookies and brownies. We keep it pretty simple. I have been thinking of adding soups and coffees though."

"Do you run the Willow Tree Sweet Shoppe? Up on Main Street? Cookie's my aunt. She told me she was fixin' to make some brownies for your shop."

"Yep, that's me. I inherited the little shop from my grandfather. He named it after me so I guess he decided I should have it. I'll fix up the shop, once I have enough time and funds."

"Sugar, you're Mr. Dixon's grandbaby. I should have seen it. You sure do take after him.

Good heavens, it's a small world we live in. My papaw used to take me in your shop for an ice cream cone every time I'd come to visit. I always wondered how it got its name. I'd look around for a weepin' willow and just be confounded. I guess now I know." Molly looked pensive then continued. "I opened me up a café once upon a time. It didn't make it though. Cookie helped me out with my sweets too. She sure does love to be in that kitchen of hers." She sighed. "I guess that's how life goes. Not everything works out." She waited while Willow sympathized with her then told Willow, "Cookie'll be around with the dishes to serve the judges." Molly moved on to the next station while Willow got things organized.

Willow transferred her chili to the chafing dish provided and lit the sterno. "This is a handy little gadget." She adjusted the heat then made sure the containers Cookie gave her corresponded to the number assigned her. All was well so she sat down and waited.

The Judging wouldn't begin for a couple of hours and she was free to do as she pleased. She elected to stay with her chili, as any smart cook would do. A person never knew what a desperate entrant would do to win. Willow had her heart set on participating in the national chili cook-off but was working up to it. When that day came, she'd have to prepare her chili on site in 3 to 4 hours. Talk about stress. This time she got to prepare the evening before. She was thankful for baby steps.

Willow was just about to start reading the newest addition of Cooks Magazine when a loud shrill made her jump. She rolled her eyes. *Annabelle Butterfield. Why does she have to be here?* Willow had had the privilege of making Annabelle's acquaintance at her very first cook-off—a cook-off for stew. And the word privilege was used in the broadest sense of the word.

As luck would have it, Annabelle was positioned right next to Willow. *Oh great!* "Hi, Annabelle." She tried to find a smidgeon of excitement to taint her voice with. She found none. Not that Annabelle noticed.

"I should have known I'd be by the Yankee. Do they even know how to make chili up there?"

Be quiet, Willow. You don't want to go there. Not now. "You have such a sense of humor, Anna. I'm not sure how you do it."

"Sweetie, my name is Annabelle. It's one word. Not two." She tilted her head. "It's a traditional Southern name. We don't name our children after trees here in the south. That is just so sad. Bless your heart."

The way Annabelle spread out each of her syllables drove Willow crazy. And she wasn't so new to the south that she was fooled, even for a minute, by that "bless your heart." Coming from a Southern Belle, that phrase was poison. She could only imagine the animosity coming from Annabelle had to do with Willow taking second place at the last competition and Annabelle taking third. Good thing she hadn't won. Who knows how Annabelle would have reacted. "Well, where I'm from we don't run our first and middle names together. It just isn't done."

Annabelle turned her nose up. Just enough to be noticed by Willow but not enough to compromise her Southern manners. That wouldn't do. "Silly, Annabelle is my first name. My middle name is Josephine. We may be Southerners but we are refined Southerners."

Willow lost it. Her laugh nearly brought tears as well as the attention of everyone in the room. Annabelle turned, as she would say in her most "refined" Southern accent, scarlet. Willow howled. She noticed Annabelle turn her attention to her chili. *Good. Maybe she'll leave me alone.*

The room was filling up with contestants preparing their chili. Willow was halfway through her magazine, thankfully read in relative peace and quiet, when Molly started the announcements and the judge introductions. She stood up to get a better view. These three judges held her culinary contest fate in their hands. She had to see what they looked like.

The first two she recognized as judges from the first contest she entered. Mr. Beau Lovett, food connoisseur and critic, was the first introduction. He had been rather lavish with his praise for her stew, Booyah, a traditional Belgium stew still enjoyed where she was from in Wisconsin. Mr. Richard B. Sutton, the second judge, owned and operated the best barbecue restaurant south of the mason Dixon line. Or so they say. He too judged Willow's stew and found it pleasant, but lacking kick. He wouldn't be able to say that about her chili. No, sir. She stretched her neck to see who the third judge was. She was about to take a drink of her soda when Ms. Delonda Posey, popular Southern food vlogger and the inspiration behind A Southern Woman's Daily Table, a column in the local newspaper, was introduced.

Willow's sharp intake of air, the *kerplunk* of the can hitting the cafeteria floor, fizzing, twirling, and spraying everything and everyone in shooting distance, could be heard all across the room. Enough so even the hostess and the judges stopped to see what was going on.

Ms. Posey started with the can bouncing around the room then rested her eyes on the face of Willow. She was silent for a nano second before she pointed her finger and yelled in a deep guttural Southern voice. "You! It's you!"

Willow brought her phone to her face and looked from the picture on the screen to the woman standing in the front of the room. "Oh dear, Lord. It's her." She mumbled. Her feet and legs turned to lead. She tried to move, she really did. But, her bottom extremities were not cooperating. The soda can finally came to a rest.

Annabelle was screaming the loudest. "You ruined my dress. You bumbling idiot." She was frantically dabbing at her newly formed brown spots with her proper southern handkerchief.

Willow finally found her feet and began to back up. She spotted the nearest exit and made a run for it. She ran all the way to her Jeep before she realized—*she can't kill me in public, too many witnesses. My chili!*

Willow ran right back into the building and stood next to her chili. The judges were already seated and Ms. Posey could do nothing but glare. Willow swallowed hard. Thank God this was a blind taste test. The woman would never know which chili was hers.

Willow watched as the judges tasted bowl after bowl of chili. They would talk among themselves then make notes on their scorecards.

The chili bowls were numbered then scrambled so no one knew whose chili the judges were tasting.

All of a sudden, Ms. Posey grabbed her throat and thrashed for a few seconds. Before Willow knew what was happening, the woman who nearly killed her was face down dead in a bowl of chili.

Chapter 3

Willow watched as the whole place went crazy. The hostess, Molly, was trying to dial on her cell phone and the other two judges were desperately trying to perform CPR on the woman, but mostly getting in each other's way. Cookie was wailing like banshee. And to make matters worse, Annabelle, fainted. But the judge was already dead. *Dead, dead.* How could someone die so quick? For the second time that day Willow was unable to move.

There was a dead body on the platform, in the middle of a chili cook-off. Right here in the little town of Turtle, Oklahoma. Where nothing happened. *How could this happen?*

The police chief finally arrived and picked up the bowl of chili with glove laden hands. He peered at the number underneath then spoke with the hostess. They both looked out at the contestants. It seemed every contestant was holding their breath. No one knew whose chili, if anyone's, killed the judge.

Willow snuck a glance around the room. A few of the cooks were talking quietly among themselves. Willow stood by herself, waiting for the news. *Perhaps she died from natural causes?* Willow didn't think so. She was too fired up to be sick. And too feisty to let a disease take her down. The question of the hour appeared to be, who killed the judge and why?

One by one, each of the chili cooks were taken into a separate room and questioned. Finally, it was Willow's turn.

"Ms. Crier, I'm Police Chief Grice. I'd like to ask you a few questions."

Not trusting her voice, she nodded. This was her first encounter with the city police chief. He was at least 40, although he could have easily passed for 35. When he smiled, his dimple caught her by surprise. His blond hair was cut short, a little too short in her opinion. He was fit and at least six foot. Which was good because she was 5'9". She wondered where that came from and why it mattered.

"Did you know the deceased?"

She shook her head, not really hearing the question while looking into those deep blue eyes.

He studied her. "Are you sure? You've never met the deceased?"

Willow remembered her earlier encounter with the judge. Her eyes widened.

"Yes, I thought so. Ms. Crier, I'm going to need you to tell me how you met the victim."

Victim? So something sinister did take place here today. She took a drink of water then retold her one and only encounter with Ms. Posey, starting at the very beginning the day before and ending with sitting in the chair before him.

"You had no idea Ms. Posey was a judge in today's cook-off?"

"No, I didn't. I was so surprised I dropped my soda when she was introduced. I didn't know who the judges were. Not until right before the judging started."

"Well, Ms. Crier, it was your chili Ms. Posey ended up face down in."

Willow gasped. "What? Did she have a heart attack? Was she sick? I know it wasn't my chili. I had a bowl for lunch and I'm fine."

"We aren't sure yet what caused her demise. In the meantime, I don't want you leaving town." He took her hand and held it a fraction of a moment too long. She was certain her imagination wasn't playing tricks on her. His smile confirmed it. He was flirting with her. "I'm sure we'll be talking soon, Ms. Crier."

Willow returned the smile. "Please, call me Willow." She handed him a Willow Tree Sweet Shoppe business card.

"Willow it is. I'll be talking with you soon." He let go of her hand and walked her to the door.

Willow left in her jeep with a lot less to carry than when she had arrived. The police officers took everything from her station. Nothing was left behind. It all had to be tested. Everyone's chili had to be tested. The police chief said, "Just in case." Her question was, *"Just in case of what? Poison? E.coli? Salmonella? Certainly not!"* At least hers wasn't the only chili to be singled out.

Chapter 4

Willow was glad to see Embry's car in the driveway. Her daughter was working as a waitress in downtown Oklahoma City. She liked the big city. Willow did not. This suited them both. Embry had a small apartment in the city and came out when she needed to breathe some fresh country air, or she needed something from her mom, which ever came first. Willow hoped today was a fresh country air day. She wasn't sure if she had the stamina for anything else.

She opened the door and the burn of chili peppers assaulted her nose. Embry found the chili she'd saved for supper.

"Mom, this stuff rocks." She said in-between bites.

Willow tossed her purse down on the coffee table and plopped down next to her daughter.

"You okay? Didn't you win? I can't imagine what the winning chili tasted like if you didn't win. That stuff must be off the charts cause this is the best chili I've ever eaten."

"Nope, I didn't win. In fact, I didn't even place. Because the cook-off got cancelled. Why?" She asked with sarcasm before answering her own question. "Because remember that woman who was road rage central yesterday?"

Willow waited for Embry to nod.

"Well, she was a judge."

"Oh no, Mom. You've got to be kidding me. What are the odds?"

"Oh, that's not the best part. The best part is, she dropped dead after taking a bite of my chili. One bite. Face dive right into the bowl."

Embry pushed the bowl away from her. "Sheesh, Ma, you could have told me this before I ate half a bowl full."

"The chili is fine. I had a bowl for lunch. I'm still living."

Embry took the bowl back. "Okay, I'll trust you." She took another bite. "Wait a minute. You mean the lady who went postal on you yesterday…the same lady you took pictures of and put them on your Facebook wall, is dead? From eating your chili?"

"Yeah, I mean no. I don't know. It could have been anyone's chili. Now you're getting the picture."

She spoke with her mouth full. "See what happens when you instigate? Not only could she have had a gun and shot you, but she could end up dead with a face full of your chili. You should have just ignored her. At least you wouldn't have a string of pictures on Facebook incriminating you. Now what are you going to do?"

"I don't know."

"What do you mean you don't know? You're going to investigate. You're going to prove it wasn't you. With all the evidence stacked up against you, you gotta do something."

Embry pulled her laptop out of its case and typed in the name Willow provided, Delonda Posey. Willow nudged closer so she could see the screen. The woman had made enough people mad, that was for sure. Her Facebook page alone was a gold mine. Now who and why. She already knew the when. Her chili and her mantle's lack of a trophy would testify to that.

Embry found Delonda's vlog with ease and watched the several posts. She had video of home cooked dishes being prepared, interviews with unsuspecting restaurateurs, chefs who needed to be put in their place, and local businesses that had received a rating in the Delonda Rating System, some of which were brutal. She even secretly recorded trips to restaurants and local food businesses and had the gall to post the recordings on her vlog, especially the ones in which she got into an altercation with the owner over how a certain dish is prepared or the service she received.

Willow's mouth dropped when she saw an argument between Delonda and Richard Sutton, the other judge who owned the Barbecue restaurant, nearly come to blows. "We have our work cut out for us. This could be anyone's doing."

Embry patted her mom's knee. "I have off tomorrow. Want me to come in to the shop with you? We could dish up ice cream and make a list. I'll bring my laptop. You got wireless internet installed, right?" She quickly added. "And we need to get back into the high school and peek around. Maybe somebody missed something."

"Yes and yes. It's been in for a couple of weeks now. And I'd love to dish ice cream with you and make a list. Maybe Police Chief Grice will have an update by then. If you're at the shop, I could run down to the police station and check on things."

"Great idea, Mom." Embry looked a little closer. "Mom, did you just smile when you said the police chief's name?"

"Why would I do that?"

Embry narrowed her eyes. "Mom? Fess up."

"Oh, Embry. There isn't anything to tell. Except he has a smile that could knock a girl off balance. I will say that much."

"Oh? Tell me more."

Much later, Willow slipped into her bed thinking about a pair of dark blue eyes, a wide pair of shoulders, and a dimple that only she could see.

Her dreams on the other hand had her running for her life from a smoked pig wielding a knife. She woke up with the name Richard Sutton on her lips. Perhaps revenge was the why and could the "who" be Richard Sutton? She looked at the clock. 5:30. She didn't have to set an alarm when she only sold ice cream. Now that she added sweets to the menu, she had to go in a bit earlier and stay later to get her baking done. If she added coffee, it would mean an even earlier day. *A girl has to earn a living.*

She flipped on the news and there she was. In all of her glory. Taking pictures from the safety of her jeep while a woman taunted her. Not just any woman. A woman who was most certainly murdered. She realized several people videoed her interaction with Ms. Posey but who already knew about her murder? And who wanted to make sure Willow was the first in line to take the blame?

Chapter 5

Willow's phone started ringing shortly after the newscast ended. Her best friend, Janie, was the first to get through.

"Did you see yourself on the news?" Janie was a morning person. Somehow, their friendship survived.

"Yes, I did." After explaining the whole sordid ordeal, Janie insisted on joining her and Embry at the shop, even though it was her day off. The "three heads are certainly better than two" argument won out.

By nine o'clock all three ladies were gathered around one of the café style tables in Willow Tree Sweets Shoppe brainstorming. The place was decorated like an old time soda fountain shop. Her grandfather's doing. She wanted to update the décor but hadn't gotten around to it yet. It still had red and white striped curtains, an ice cream counter with red topped round bar stools, a black and white checked floor, even a candy counter. Willow had installed a case for the baked items but that was about it. If she decided to add specialty coffees she would need to invest more money in the shop. She had to figure this murder out so she would feel comfortable making it her own. Until then, she was stuck. She had to save where she could.

Willow wasn't even sure the woman was murdered. She could have had a heart attack. Willow started to declare the whole gathering of the minds a waste of time when police chief Grice opened the door.

Willow frowned. Not one small glimpse of that dimple. It must be bad news.

"Can we talk for a minute?"

"Sure. Let's go back to my office."

Embry started humming *He's So Fine* and Willow gave her a look to shut her up. Not that it worked.

Willow closed the door once they both managed to finagle themselves in her tiny cubicle of an office.

Police Chief Grice took off his hat. "Good morning, Ms. Crier."

"It's Willow, remember?"

Yes, Willow. Um, call me Steve." He smiled and revealed the sweet dimple she so wanted to see then he quickly went straight faced. "Well, it's official. Ms. Posey was murdered. She had a severe reaction to peanuts. She was highly allergic.

Someone with that information used it to murder the food columnist. Our medical examiner found traces of peanuts in her stomach contents."

Willow leaned back against her desk and pictured the stomach content scenes in crime scene shows, labs, and gothic lab assistants testing food. She nodded her head. "I was afraid of that. You don't know whose chili it was yet, do you?"

"No, those tests won't be back for a few days." He looked a bit nervous. "I saw the news this morning. And I saw your posts on Facebook. You seem to have put yourself right in the middle of a murder."

"It would appear that way, wouldn't it?" Willow sighed. "There is only one thing I can do."

Grice raised his eyebrows.

"Solve it."

"Ms. Crier, I mean, Willow, I think it best if you leave the murder solving business to the professionals. One person has already been murdered. We don't need another body showing up. And certainly not yours."

Willow watched the police chief's face turn bright red.

"I mean, we don't want anyone else hurt. No one, including you."

"Chief Grice, I'm a newcomer here. People don't know me yet. I have a business to run and that business won't support itself. If the town doesn't trust me, they won't buy my goods. If they don't buy my goods, I'm outta business." Willow stood up. "And I cannot let that happen. I won't let it happen. My grandfather spent his entire life serving this town his very favorite treat. I won't let anything happen to this shop."

"Promise me you'll be careful. And if you find anything out, come to me first."

Willow nodded. "Okay, well, we already have a suspect."

"We?"

"Yes, my daughter, Embry, and my best friend, Janie. We're making a list of suspects now. Did you know that Richard Sutton got into a heated argument with the deceased and she posted the argument on her vlog?"

"Vlog? What is a vlog?"

"Oh, it's like a blog but instead of writing an article, you use video." She opened the door. "Come on, I'll show you."

"I have to be honest. I don't even know what a blog is."

"You're not on the computer much, are you?"

He shook his head. "Well, not outside of work. I have to be on the darn thing so much at work I don't even own one at home. I have an old

[28]

fashioned typewriter I use for personal use. If I have to send email, I do so from work."

"You'll be a pro by the time I'm done with you. Or perhaps I should say when Embry is finished with you. She's my go-to girl for anything computer related."

Janie and Embry were still watching posts on Delonda's website when Willow and Chief Grier rejoined them.

"Hey guys, bring up that post with Richard Sutton again. Steve wants to see it."

Embry smiled at the use of the police chief's first name. "Okay, mom. I'm sure Police Chief Grice will find this useful."

A few seconds later Delonda Posey was trashing the Barbecue Palace like it was the worst dining establishment on the face of the earth. She even went so far as to say that Richard stole his barbecue recipe. That is when things really got ugly. Of course Willow experienced Delonda's "ugly" during a fit of road rage. Using video to trash someone's means of supporting themselves was a whole other form of ugly. And it would appear Delonda had no issue with that kind of ugly.

Richard was screaming he would sue her. She was shouting her right to free speech. Customers and employees were holding them both back and the police ended up escorting Delonda out of the restaurant. And she was banned for life.

Willow speculated. "I'm betting Richard didn't know she was videotaping the whole thing. Or having someone else do her dirty work for her. He couldn't have. He must have been livid when he found out." She thought back to the judge introductions. "And how they could have been so cordial to one another on that platform is beyond me. And why were they both judges for this competition? Surely someone knew they were enemies."

Steve saw the validity in her questions. "It would seem that someone at the chili cook-off did the deed. They had the means and the opportunity."

"Yes. Richard seems the obvious choice. But I'm guessing she made enemies of a lot more people than just Richard. The question becomes…how many of her enemies were also at the cook off?"

The front door bell tinkled and all four looked up.

Willow rolled her eyes. *Annabelle*. Two days in a row was more than anyone could handle. Entering right behind her was Molly. Molly on the other hand, put a smile on Willow's face. It was good to see the contest hostess again.

"What brings you two in here this morning?"

Annabelle answered. "Scones. We need scones for our morning Bible study. The store I normally get them from is out. So that left you. I wouldn't have come in for the world but Molly insisted we give yours a try. I have no doubt they will leave me wanting." She turned to Molly. "I'm sure the little ones won't care where they get their cookies from. Their taste buds are not quite developed just yet." She turned back to Willow. "I'll take two dozen of your cut out cookies as well."

Willow wanted to throw her southern backside out the door but a dozen scones and two dozen cookies would help today's bottom line. And judging from the line extending out the door, rather, the lack of one, this might be today's grand bottom line. She opened two boxes and arranged the scones and cookies.

Annabelle wandered to where the police chief, Janie, and Embry sat. "So, I heard she was murdered. I also heard it was Beau Lovett. They had a big falling out a little while back. Rumor has it he vowed he would pay her back."

Willow wanted to ask her how spreading rumors and Bible studies mixed but kept her trap shut. Wasn't gossip a no-no? Instead, she let the chief answer.

"Yes, it would appear someone wanted to get revenge." He stood up and made for the door. "And it's my job to find who that someone is." He nodded in the direction of Willow, replaced his hat and left. Leaving no doubt whatsoever in any of the ladies' minds he meant business.

Annabelle turned to Willow. "Of course the first person on the suspect list is you, Willow. Did you really let yourself be recorded for national television without a single drop of makeup on? Honey, you really should pick up some good makeup. And make sure you get some bb cream. It will help fill in all those little lines by your eyes." She moved her finger around, as if she was applying the make-up herself. "We Southern women wouldn't be caught dead outside our bedrooms without our face properly applied. Heaven forbid. Someone might come over." She shook her head in exasperation. "The horror. Being caught on television 'au natural.' Goodness." Annabelle turned to Molly. "The things we must teach those who didn't have the good fortune of a proper upbringing." She paid her bill and started for the door. "Come, Molly. We mustn't be late."

Annabelle was gone before Willow could form a response. She sat down next to her daughter and all three ladies busted out in laughter.

Chapter 6

Willow remembered why they were gathered at her shop and sobered up. "We need a way to get everyone who was at the chili cook-off together so we can interact with them. There must be something we can do."

Embry's eyebrows shot up. "Mom, what if we hosted everyone out at the ranch? Maybe a commemorative get together to remember Ms. Posey by."

Janie added. "We could even ask Molly about re-doing the chili cook-off. I bet she would be all for it. I'm guessing everyone would come. Even the killer. They would have to come or they would look guilty."

Willow nodded. "That's a really good idea, you two. I'll give Molly a call later this afternoon when I know she'll be finished with her Bible study. Of course it means I'll have to enjoy the presence of Annabelle once more, but what can I do?" She paused and blushed a little. "I'll have to run it by Chief Grice as well."

Embry grinned. "So, it's chief now. What happened to Steve?"

Willow tapped her shoulder playfully. "That's enough out of you!" She was back to business. "We'll all need to be there to keep our eyes and ears open. Will that work?"

Janie answered first. "I don't know. I think I'm scheduled to work that day. I'll have to check with my boss."

Willow chuckled. "I have a firm in with the boss. I think you'll be fine." She turned to Embry. "What about you? Don't you have to work at the restaurant on Saturday?"

"I'll get someone to cover for me. I've done so many favors they all owe me. Someone should be available."

"Okay, as long as Molly is okay with it and the Chief gives me his okay, we're on. I'll have our part time girl cover the shop. Heaven knows we haven't had much business since the murder. She should be able to handle it."

Surprisingly, a few people ventured into the shop over lunch time. Willow guessed they wanted to see who the number one murder suspect was, because they sure didn't buy much. A cookie or a muffin and a couple of bottles of water. Something had to change quickly or she'd be in the hole faster than the gopher living in her front yard.

In between customers, Willow made a list of everyone she remembered being at the cook-off. She left a message on Molly's voicemail asking her to call then got busy making the dough for tomorrow's banana bread. The town loved her banana bread. Probably the chocolate chips and nuts she added. Maybe the smell alone would bring them in droves. At least she hoped so.

Embry reminded Willow of the quick trip across town that was needing their attention. Willow glanced at the empty tables and told Janie where they were going. The high school.

Willow drove around to the back of the school, near to where the cafeteria was located. She parked by the back door and gave it a pull. She was surprised it was open. She opened the door then nodded to Embry, giving her the all clear signal. Which really looked like a "come on, hurry up, arm flying, child motivating move from their days as a mother and young daughter. Some things never change.

They both moved quietly through the dimly lit cafeteria and into the better lit kitchen. Thankfully, no one was around. Willow moved the trash can, looking for anything that might have been missed by the police chief. Nothing.

Embry started looking in nooks and crannies that might have been overlooked. She just knew the killer had to have hid some evidence to get rid of later. They needed a place that would have been easily accessed and that no one would have thought to look in. She fully expected to find some trace of peanuts, perhaps even a wrapper or a baggie. The killer had to have carried the peanuts in something. She moved into the pantry to search further.

Willow opened the coffee canister and was about to dig in when she heard a very profound harrumph behind her. She turned to see who had caught her in the act. Police Chief Grice was standing 10 feet behind her with his hands on his hips.

"What are you doing here?"

Willow looked from the coffee can to the chief. "Um, looking for clues?"

"In the coffee?"

"Well, we kind of figured…"

The chief interrupted. "We?"

Embry stuck her head around the pantry door and smiled. "Hi."

He waved. "Okay, I got the we…go ahead."

Willow continued. "As I was saying, we kind of figured the killer had to of stashed something contaminated here at the school. If they had peanuts on them, you would have found the evidence during the search and questioning. But, I'm guessing you didn't. That means, it must be here. Something has to be. It just didn't get up and walk away."

"Yes, I was kind of thinking along those lines myself. We didn't find any storage containers or bags with peanuts in it. And the tests aren't back yet on whether or not the pots of chili had peanuts. The peanuts could have been added to the pots, although why the killer would incriminate himself like that, I have no idea. They could have also been added to the dishes the judges were served out of."

Willow let out a gasp. "Cookie is the one who passed those dishes out. And she helps out here for lunch...you don't think...?" She let her thought fall off. Cookie wasn't a murderer. She was in her early 60's. Old women didn't murder people? Or did they?

The chief picked up where Willow left off. "If it was her, she would have had ample opportunity to get rid of the evidence."

Just then Embry let out a yell. "I found something!"

Both the Police Chief and Willow moved quickly to the pantry door.

He spoke first. "Don't touch anything." Then looked over her shoulder to see what she had found. There, in the nestled pots, she found a baggie with what looked like crumbs in it.

Willow looked on as well. "I bet you a hundred bucks that's ground peanuts."

The chief put on a pair of gloves and removed the bag. He also took the pile of nesting pots. All three turned around to see Cookie standing in the open doorway, staring at them.

"What is going on in my kitchen?"

She had become somewhat possessive of the high school kitchen. Willow wondered why. "Hello, Cookie. I didn't know you were still here." She glanced at her watch. It was after four.

"Of course I'm still here. I work here. And I have some prep work to do for tomorrow's lunch."

She looked at the pots in the chief's hands. "And where do you think you're going with my pots?"

"I just need to dust these pots for fingerprints then you can have them back, I promise. We found some evidence here. Something to do with Ms. Posey's murder." He went on. "You know I have to do everything I can to find the killer."

Willow was surprised to hear the chief talking the way he was to Cookie. Yes, she was the town's matriarch, but he was the chief. And there was a murderer to find. Surely he wasn't going to ignore the evidence—even if it did implicate the town's best baker. Because doing so meant for every step forward Willow made in finding the killer, the chief took one step back. That wasn't going to help her clear herself. Not in the least.

He gave her an "I'm sorry" shrug and loaded up the newly found evidence and carted it off to the police station.

Embry dropped Willow off at the ice cream shop and told her she would ask around at work to see if there was any information worthy of repeating. The restaurant business was a tight group and word usually got around. She would do her best to find out something.

After returning, Willow was about to send Janie out the door when her cell phone rang. She recognized the number. Molly.

"Hey, Molly. Would you have a few minutes to stop into the shop? I'd like to talk to you about an idea I'm having."

Molly agreed and Willow asked Janie to mix the dough for her famous chocolate chip cookies while she sat down with Molly. Willow poured a couple of glasses of sweet tea and waited for

Molly. The church she attended was only a few blocks away so she knew it wouldn't be more than a couple of minutes. She quickly got up and put a few treats on a plate. *Might as well butter her up. I really need this to work.*

The bell on the door tinkled just as Willow was returning to her seat. She stood again. "Hi, Molly. Thanks for coming over. I figured you might need something to drink." She offered her the glass and snacks before coming right to the point.

Molly seemed upset with Willow's idea. "Don't you think it's a mite too soon? That we're being disrespectful if we put on the chili cook-off now? I mean, the poor woman's just passed."

"No. I really don't. Besides, from everything I have learned about Delonda she would want to be in the spot light, even in death."

It took some convincing but Molly was on board. Especially since Willow would provide the place. Molly was already out the money for renting the high school cafeteria. The money from community sales would have helped cover those costs—and normally did, but not with these circumstances. Everyone had gone home and took their money with them.

Willow convinced her that at least by rescheduling she would be saving face with the entrants. Someone would take a trophy home and everyone would be more apt to enter the next cook-off. She hoped. It was the deciding factor. Molly promised to get a list together of everyone who entered and volunteered for the cook-off. She said she would even make phone calls and invite them all to the makeup date.

Willow thanked Molly and called Chief Grice as soon as she was out the door. "Hi, Chief. Do you have time to meet with me this afternoon or evening? I have an idea I want to discuss with you."

He cleared his throat. "Yeah, I have some time when I get off, say around six? Do you want to grab a bite to eat? We could talk then. I have some news myself."

Willow swallowed hard. Was he asking her on a date? She jumped on that. "Oh, well, sure. I'll be home by then but I could meet you back in town at the shop if that would be easier?"

"It's no problem. I'll pick you up at your place."

"Okay. See you tonight." Only after she hung up did she remember he had news to share as well. She was a basket of nerves all day while baking and restocking the shops shelves. She made a couple of milk shakes for the after school crowd and served up some sundaes and a few cones. It appeared the kids didn't mind she was a murder suspect. As long as she was still serving treats, they would be there to eat them up.

Chapter 7

Willow rushed home to get ready for her date. Well, it wasn't really a date. Just because the chief was hungry after work, and just because he did ask her to get a bite, didn't make it a date. In fact, he was probably just killing two birds with one stone by eating and hearing what she had to say. She guessed the chief would pick a casual dining setting so she chose a pair of jeans and light blue sweater. The sweater really popped with her dark hair hanging down. She touched up the little make-up she wore, even though Annabelle insisted she didn't know how to apply it, and put on some lip gloss. She had always liked the more natural look. The men she dated didn't seem to mind. Ah well, to each her own.

Willow walked around her house. It was fairly large. Three big bedrooms, one of which she used as an office. The master had its own bath with a soaking tub which she absolutely took advantage of on cooler evenings. Although the kitchen needed updating, it had good bones. Her grandfather had envisioned an open concept before they were popular so the kitchen opened up to the living and dining rooms. She loved that about the house. She could have people over and cook while still taking part in the conversation and activities. It would make hosting the chili cook-off that much more appealing.

Her house was brick, like most of the houses around. Kept the place cooler in the summer. Or so they say. Summer was coming so she'd find out. The best part of her place was the land. She had 25 acres. The dirt was orange. The trees were sparse. Water was a foreign commodity. But it was land. And it was hers. Something she could pass down to her daughter. And someday her grandchildren would get it. She loved the idea of that. She heard a vehicle coming down her driveway and stepped out on her big front porch and waved.

Willow locked her front door and walked toward the passenger side of Steve's truck. He jumped out before she reached the door and opened it for her. "Chivalry isn't dead in the south, is it?" She smiled and thanked him.

He climbed in next to her. "Not if I can help it. And most the men who live here. Our mamas have taught us well."

She smiled and got a dimple as a reward. She could look at that face all day long. She prayed he couldn't read her thoughts.

"Nice place you got here. Does your daughter live with you?"

"Nope, she's got a place in the city. I'm the country girl in the family."

His face clouded over and his dimple disappeared. "I'm not sure I like you being out here all by yourself. Now with a killer on the loose. Do you have a dog?"

"Nope again. I've been wanting to get to the shelter but their hours coincide with my shop's hours. I haven't been able to make it in." She grinned. "But you don't have to worry. I fully believe in the second amendment. I have a shot gun, a stun gun, and pepper spray. I just got my concealed carry permit and I'll be packing before long." She smiled, obviously proud of herself.

"Think of a dog as a warning siren. He will let you know if anything or anyone who shouldn't be on your property is approaching." He made a face. "Huh. Change of plans. Do you like hot dogs?"

"Give me a Chicago style hot dog any day of the week and I'll be a happy camper."

"Well, I'm not sure if they have Chicago style dogs, but their dogs are pretty darn good.

You'll see." He made a U-turn in the middle of the road and took off in the opposite direction. 15 minutes later he pulled up in front of a little road side shack and ordered a couple of dogs, with everything, and two cans of coke.

Willow watched her romantic dinner go down the drain. Even so, she smiled and took a bite of her hot dog. He just watched her.

After she swallowed her first bite, and he still hadn't touched his, she paused. "I should have waited. I'm sorry." She wiped her mouth with her napkin. "I will say this is pretty darn good."

He smiled. "It's okay. Do you mind if I say a quick prayer before I eat?"

She shook her head no.

He prayed silently then took a bite of his own hot dog. "What did I tell ya? They are some kind of good." He finished his dog then took off heading in the same direction. A few miles down the road he turned into a driveway. A really nice driveway. He helped her from the truck then led the way to a lovely country home.

Willow wondered who lived here. She didn't have to wait long to find out.

A tall, thin, well dressed woman came out the front door to greet Steve. "Steve, what are you doing here?"

She hugged him and kissed his cheek. Willow felt her face flush so she turned the other way. She had no right to be jealous, but she couldn't help it. In a few, short days' time she had become somewhat possessive of her police chief. She heard her name.

"Willow, this is my sister, Beth. Beth, this is Willow. She is Old man Peter's granddaughter and she took over the ice cream shop. She's living at his ranch on the other side of town." He smiled. "All alone."

Beth nodded. "Of course she is. I could have guessed." She stuck her hand out. "Nice to meet you, Willow. Any friend of Steve's is a friend of ours. Come on in. I'll introduce you to the rest of the family."

Willow entered the grand home and was instantly greeted by the "family." There must have been at least six dogs gathered at her feet, wanting attention. All different shapes and sizes, and by the looks of them, mostly mixed breeds.

Beth bent down. "I operate a re-homing shelter out of my house. We have placed quite a few dogs this way. I have friends in the city who keep me in constant supply. The shelters are so full and are having a hard time placing their dogs so this is how I help. Instead of leaving these little guys wandering the streets, they get to come live with me. My brother helps me place them. He has a soft heart." She gave him a side hug. "And if they never find a home, then this becomes their permanent home. My husband knew when he married me that I was a sucker for these guys. He has accepted his fate. And don't let him fool you. He may seem tough with them but he loves them as much as I do."

She led them into the kitchen where she was putting the finishing touches on a salad. "Don't tell me he took you to that hot dog stand for supper." She rolled her eyes when Willow confirmed. "Well, you'll eat a proper supper with us."

Willow watched Steve's face light up. He had been counting on this, she could tell. Without taking her eyes off of Steve's face, she asked. "Does he do this sort of thing often?"

Beth smiled. "Show up for supper or bring ladies in need of protecting?"

Willow cocked her head. "Both?"

Beth laughed. "More often than not for supper and only when the situation warrants it for the latter. I told you he has a heart for these little guys, right?"

Even with the hot dog, Willow could still manage to eat. Especially with food that smelled out of this world. Besides, she never pretended she wasn't hungry. She could put away food with the best of the men. "Can I help with anything?"

"You can grab a couple more plates out of the cupboard to the left of the sink. Silverware is in the drawer underneath. Steve, would you get two glasses out and fill them with ice."

Both Willow and Steve moved quickly. Beth was putting dinner on the table and both were anticipating a better offering than a roadside hotdog.

Willow breathed the enticing smells in deeply as Garrett, Beth's husband, took his place at the head of the table.

"I see we have guests for dinner. Steve, did you smell lasagna from the other side of town? I don't think you've ever missed a lasagna dinner." He laughed a hearty, belly laugh.

Willow instantly liked him. And if she had the option, she wouldn't miss one either. She had learned her lesson with the hotdog and didn't put a morsel of food in her mouth until those providing the food started eating. Just like Steve, they prayed before they ate. She was learning this was a regular occurrence of people who lived in Oklahoma. She didn't mind. She wasn't raised in the church but she was raised to respect God and prayer was a part of that. She closed her eyes and joined them. The prayer was short. Apparently Garrett was hungry.

She took a bite of the piping hot lasagna just as Garrett asked her a question. "So, my wife tells me you are in need of a guard dog."

She was trying to move the food around and not burn her tongue. She swallowed too quickly and thought steam must have come out of her ears. She guzzled some tea before answering.

Steve was still blowing on his first fork full. "Be careful, it's hot."

Willow gave him a dirty look then answered Garrett. "I've been thinking about it for a while. I wouldn't mind having a companion. I wouldn't say I need a guard dog though. I think Steve is worried for nothing." She started blowing on another fork full of food. "Besides, I told him I have all sorts of protective devices. An intruder will see the end of my shotgun if he tries to get in my house."

Garrett laughed. "I like you. Aren't you supposed to be a Yankee? I didn't think Yankee's liked guns."

"You've got me mixed up with a liberal Yank. We're two different breeds."

He laughed again. "I really like you. Where'd you find this girl, Steve? You've got to keep her." He took a drink of his tea and continued. "Think of it this way. A dog tells you when to load your gun. How does that sound?"

"I like it. Good point." She could tell Steve and Garrett were related, even if only by marriage.

She looked around for the dogs and all six of them were lined up at the living room door with their noses directly on the line separating the two rooms. "Wow, they are well behaved."

Garrett responded, "They know they won't have a home for long if they don't obey the rules. No dogs at the table."

Willow, remembering what was said before dinner, looked at Beth who only responded with a raise of her eyebrows and a sly grin. He was certainly all talk. Even so, the dogs were well behaved.

The four of them finished supper and Steve and Willow helped clear the table. Working together things were cleared quickly and Willow found herself on the living room floor playing with the dogs. One in particular captured her heart. She looked to be a mix breed of lab, rot, and possibly shepherd. She took to Willow as well and didn't leave her side for the remainder of her visit.

"I guess we know which dog I'm taking." She hugged the puppy on her lap.

Steve asked to talk to Beth privately and left Willow to fend for herself for a few minutes.

When they returned, Beth had a leash in her hand and Steve carried some food and a couple of dog dishes.

"Beth is going to bend the rules for us. You still have to fill out an application but I vouched for you. We're both assuming you aren't going to be running any dog fighting rings out at your ranch."

Willow's mouth dropped. "People still do that sort of thing? How cruel."

Steve looked at his sister. "I'll take that as a no, how about you?"

Beth nodded and attached the leash to Clover. "She will make a wonderful pet. She's such a good dog. And she's protective too. She'll get even more so as she gets older. She's only a year and a half."

After thanking Beth and Garrett for a wonderful meal, Willow and Steve loaded up the dog and her belongings and took off for Willow's place. The dog sat on Willow's lap the whole way.

"You're kind of big to be a lap dog, don't you think?" The dog's only response was to turn and lick her right up the side of her face.

Steve started laughing. "I really think she likes you." He pulled into her driveway. "You know, we never did get around to that talk."

Willow raised her hand to her mouth. "I totally forgot."

"It happens, especially when a person is enjoying what they're doing. Like we did this evening. I still have some time if you'd like to sit on the porch and let your dog study her surroundings."

"That sounds good. I've got some peach cobbler in the house if you would like some dessert."

"Oh, I'm getting spoiled. I usually warm up some leftovers or make a tv dinner. Something simple like that."

Willow returned with a tray of tea and two portions of cobbler heated up with ice cream scooped on top. She poured the tea then asked the question she needed to ask. "I'm thinking of having a commemorative re-match on the chili cook-off. Molly has already agreed but I wanted to run it by you. I'd have it here next Saturday afternoon. What do you think?"

He swallowed his tea. "You know you might be inviting her killer to your home, right?"

"Yes, but just think, I'd have everyone together from the cook-off. It might be the only way to get everyone in one place."

"It could work, but it could be dangerous. I will only approve if I can be here to watch over things."

"I figured you would say that. You can come as my date. Maybe then people won't think you're there to find a murderer."

He tilted his head. "I can live with that." He smiled the smile that stilled her heart.

She waited then asked. "Don't you have news for me?"

"Oh, yes, right. We got the tests back from the pots of chili and from the fingerprints on the pots from the school. Both are a no. No trace of peanuts in the chili and no prints on the pots. The ladies at the cafeteria regularly wear gloves so that explains why their prints are missing. The killer must have been extremely careful or have worn gloves too. They must have added the crushed peanuts to the serving bowls. The good news is, we can rule out your bowl because she would not have died instantly after taking one bite. And even though she may have been experiencing some symptoms, she might not have thought anything of it. She had a reaction earlier in the day to something she was allergic to, but not so far as being anaphylactic. My guess is she still thought she was suffering a little from her morning reaction. Her mother told us about the morning episode. It wasn't peanuts or she would have been in almost the same boat. Epi pens don't always work when the allergic reaction is severe."

Willow jumped up and down. "I'm in the clear. For sure?"

"Yeah, we pretty much ruled you out. Turns out your story matches your photos on Facebook and we could only assume that you would never have been taunting her if you knew your winning chili might have been in jeopardy. What most people thought convicted you, actually cleared you."

"I didn't think you did the social media thing." She smirked.

He laughed. "For you I made a special exception. Besides, the guys at work are the ones who were checking out your page. They just showed me the posts."

The sun was long past setting and the evening was getting quite brisk. Steve stood up and stretched. "You think you'll be okay with her tonight? You'll have to get to the store and get her a bed and more food tomorrow. Do you have time for that?"

She pet the adorable puppy next to her. "I'll make time. Of course when word gets around that I'm cleared I might be busier than expected. I wouldn't complain though. I'll run out early tomorrow morning." Willow followed his example and stood then stretched. "I think it's time to turn in."

Steve looked like he wanted to kiss her then thought better of it. "I'll see you tomorrow. Save a slice of banana bread for me."

She watched him get in his truck and drive around the circular drive way.

She brought the dog in the house, locked the door and headed for her bed. She didn't experience a single bad dream or any tossing and turning. And she stayed extra warm all night. She awoke to a lick in the face. "I guess I won't be needing a bed for you, now will I?" She laughed and held her dog close.

Chapter 8

Willow invited Clover for a ride and took off early for the pet store in the city. Embry had the day off and had come at the very questionable hour of 7 am. She wanted to meet her new "sister" and contribute to shopping for the new dog. She sat up front and discussed the progress of the case.

"Mom, I discovered a little bit of information. Apparently Beau Lovett and Delonda Posey were going to open a restaurant together. It was going to be one of these all natural, fresh, organic trendy places and the whole idea dissolved before it ever got off the ground due to Delonda changing her mind constantly. Apparently, it was Beau who put up the biggest portion of the investment. He lost everything. Every dime he put into it and she came out of it unscathed. To the say the least, he was furious. He has a very good motive for revenge."

"I would say that puts Beau at the top of our suspect list." She immediately started yelling at the guy behind her. "You idiot. Get off the road!" Willow gave the guy in the pickup truck who almost cut her off a dirty look. "Did you see that guy? He was so cutting me off in my own lane."

Embry gave her a look. "Uh, Mom. He was in his lane. There are two turn lanes here. You actually were cutting him off."

Willow looked over her shoulder at the guy who was now giving her plenty of space. "Are you sure?"

"Yeah, Mom. I'm sure. This is why you don't live in the city. You'd never survive."

"Huh. Imagine that. Two turn lanes. I didn't see the sign for two."

"It was there, Mom. You just missed it."

"Good thing my windows were up and he couldn't hear me. I'd have to apologize."

Embry just shook her head. "Perhaps you ought to consider placing orders online and having them delivered at the house. It might be easier on everyone."

"You can do that?"

"Mom, welcome to the 21st century. Yeah, you can do that."

"Even dog food?"

"Even hamburger meat."

"Seriously?"

"Seriously!"

"I'm going to have to look into that."

Willow pulled into a parking place in front of the pet store. "You ready?"

"With you, Mom. I'm not sure I'll ever be completely ready."

Willow added toys and bones to her cart as well as some treats, a collar, a leash, and a new water and food dish so she could return Beth's. She went ahead and purchased a doggie bed. Even though she had a sneaking suspicion Clover would be sleeping with her every night. She could always use it in the living room.

Willow glanced at her daughter. "You feel like taking a little detour?"

"To where?"

"Let's go snoop around Delonda's place. See if we can figure anything out."

"As in breaking and entering?"

"No, as in hoping someone is there to let us in so you can "pretend to go to the bathroom while I keep the person occupied while you are snooping" entering. More like that kind of entering."

Embry sighed. "Okay, let's give it a shot."

Willow had done her homework and knew exactly where she was going. They picked up a pie as a token offering then stood on the front porch, knocking. Finally, after several doorbell rings and several fairly hard knocks, an older woman answered the door.

"You sure are in a hurry. Got to give us older folks a little time to get to the door. We could be doing our bizness and not in a place to answer. You hearin' me girl? You know my meaning?" She held open the door then led them inside.

"Yeah, I got it. Thanks." That was one image she would have a hard time replacing. She lifted the pie up. "I got you a pie."

The woman took the pie from her and placed it on the dining room table with the other dozen or so pies. "How many pies does one old woman need?" As if remembering her manners she said. "Thanks."

"You're welcome."

"I know you didn't come here to bring me no pie. What do you want?"

Willow paused. "Want?"

"On with it, Honey. You think I don't recognize you from those videos of you with my baby. For all I know you're the one who put her in the ground. Now, out with it. What do you want?"

"I just wanted to ask you a few questions. About Delonda."

"Ask away. Everyone else has."

Embry spoke up. "May I use your restroom?"

The woman shook her head in exasperation. "It's down the hall to the left. But, like I already told you. I was doing my bizness 'fore you got here and it ain't pretty in there. Trust me."

Embry felt an involuntary shudder and suppressed an urge to throw up. "Thanks for the warning." She headed down the hallway and made a point of opening and closing the bathroom door. She peeked in the other two rooms and found what must have been Delonda's bedroom. She trusted her mother to keep the old woman busy while she snooped.

Willow continued with her questioning. "Do you know if Delonda received any threats as of late?"

"Honey, Delonda received threats on a regular basis. She wasn't very popular. I don't know why people even listened to that trash she put out on that computer."

"Does anyone stand out, like they meant to harm her?"

The woman put her hand on her chin. "Hmm, let me think. Anyone who has ever owned a restaurant would have been out to get her. Anyone who had a cooking show. A food based bizness, like a bakery or a coffee shop. She has taken down food columnists, even critics. Or heck, even a catering bizness. I remember this one little gal opened this café with catering and Delonda trash talked her so bad nobody went back. She lost her bizness. She was none too happy, I'll tell you that. But there were so many. Too many to count."

"Do you remember who that woman was?"

"No, I don't. She was some little white girl. I do know that."

Willow rolled her eyes. That accounted for more than a quarter of the city's population.

"Don't you roll your eyes at me, Missy. I'm too old for that nonsense. Besides, all you people look the same to me."

Did she really just say that? Willow hoped Embry would hurry up. She had to get out of this house. For being so successful in the food world, Delonda sure lived in a rundown neighborhood. Willow wondered about that.

"Ms. Posey, did you stand to benefit from Delonda's demise?"

"Demise? That's a bit too fancy of a word for me. Are you asking me if I got some money from her being murdered? Is that what you're asking? Do you think I killed her for a little bit of life insurance money? Or a little bit of money in the bank?"

"No, Ma'am. That's not what I'm asking."

"You sure sounded like you were asking me that."

Willow heard her daughter approach. "Mom, my stomach isn't feeling too great. Are you almost done?"

Willow stood up. "Yes, let's get you home."

She turned to Ms. Posey. "Perhaps we can discuss this another time."

She nodded. "Perhaps."

Willow and Embry opened the front door to leave as Chief Grice was raising his hand to knock.

"You two again. Let me guess. Still looking for clues?"

Willow nodded. She had been with him the evening before and never mentioned her plans for visiting Delonda's mother.

He lowered his voice. "Did you find anything?"

To this, Willow shook her head no. "A few leads to check up on. She seems to remember some white lady who was really mad at Delonda. But, since we all look alike, she can't remember who the white lady is."

He pulled her aside. "Why are you constantly one step ahead of me?"

"Because I don't have to fill out paperwork?" She shrugged her shoulders and smiled.

The chief knocked on the front door as Willow and Embry drove away.

Willow sighed a breath of relief. "I'm so glad you came out when you did. I thought I was going to get pummeled with her cane. She clearly didn't like us." Clover, who was anxiously waiting for them, gave Willow a lick on the cheek. "Did you have a good nap, Girl?" She glanced at her daughter sitting in the passenger seat. "Did you find anything?"

"Of course I did. Wait until you see what I got. I'm not sure if her mother will miss it, but I found a whole file of people she had done an exposé on. A whole file, mom. The dirt on everyone." She looked at her mother. "And just wait 'till you see who is on that list."

Chapter 9

Willow called Steve on her way home.

"Are you driving and talking on your cell phone?"

"Why, is that illegal here?"

He laughed. "No, it's not. I just wondered."

"You're on speaker. Say hi to Embry—and Clover."

"Hi, Embry. Hi, Clover. I thought you had to work this morning. I stopped in the shop for my banana bread and you weren't there. Now I know the real reason you weren't at work. So, tell me what you found. I know you found something."

"I didn't lie. I didn't find anything. But Embry did. She just told me as we were driving away. We're on our way back now. Janie covered for me so I could run a couple of errands. Meet me there when you finish up with Ms. Posey and I'll show you what I have."

"It sounds serious. I can do that."

"Good. Your second piece of bread is on me."

"Well, I should tell you, Janie told me the first piece was on you. You might want to charge me for the second."

Willow laughed. "She knows me well. I have a soft spot for law enforcement."

"All law enforcement?"

"Yep. All the boys in blue."

"I'm not sure how I feel about that."

"Just call it thankfulness."

Both of them were interrupted from a firm throat clearing.

"Oh yeah, you're on speaker and Embry's listening in. Oops."

He laughed. "Good thing she can't see the color of my face."

Embry joined in. "I can still hear the red in your voice. That's good enough, trust me."

All three laughed.

Willow pulled up in front of the shop in record time. Clover had to do her business and Embry offered to walk her. She promised she would come in when she saw the Chief pull up.

Janie had a long line of customers. What a joy to Willow's eyes. This is what she needed. Steve promised he would get the word out she had been cleared. And he had done as promised. Her customers were returning in droves. She washed her hands then hurried behind the counter to help fill orders. By the time she was finished both Embry and Steve were sitting at an empty table waiting for her.

"Looks like you won't have any excuse to leave any time soon." He gifted her with that dimple.

She nodded. "And for that, I'm so very thankful. Here is a thank you present." She placed a warm piece of chocolate chip banana bread in front of him, along with a cup of coffee.

"Why thank you. I can't get enough of this stuff. It's great."

"It's my grandmother's recipe. I inherited all her recipes. I'm having fun trying them out. Most of them have been delicious. Want to come over for dinner tomorrow evening and be my guinea pig?"

"I would love to be your taste tester. What are we having?"

"I think I shall keep it a surprise."

"You have no idea, do you?"

She laughed. "Not a clue. But, I will think of something."

"Are you two ready to look at this list? Gosh. I'm thinking I'm still in high school."

Steve got serious. "Oh, yeah, you had something to show me. I'm assuming it is this list?"

Willow gave Embry a swift kick and Embry scowled.

"Okay, let's see this list."

The list of names seemed almost like a personal vendetta. Steve glanced over the list then had to ask. "Where did you get this?"

Willow flinched. "Do you really want to know?"

"I'm not sure I do but you better tell me anyway."

"As you know one of our errands today was visiting Delonda's house. Which meant visiting her mother. They lived together. Which you also know since you were there too."

"And she gave you this list? That was awful nice of her."

This time Willow grimaced. "Well, not quite."

He narrowed his eyes. "What do you mean, not quite?"

"Well, while I questioned her, Embry searched Delonda's room."

Steve shook his head. "So, you took this without her permission."

Willow nodded. "Yep, that about sums it up."

"You know this evidence can't be used now, right?"

"We'll just have to get the goods on the killer another way. At least we have a list of names to go by. This helps a lot."

He agreed.

They looked at the names and some of them took the trio quite by surprise. Janie even found a moment to look over Willow's shoulder. All three of the ladies gasped when they saw Annabelle's name on the list. Willow saw it first. "Annabelle? What food business was she in?"

Embry filled her in. "Look at Delonda's notes. Annabelle made candy. Turns out she particularly liked making fudge. Delonda took her down and hard. Look at this. This says her chocolate was grainy. Her fudge didn't have enough flavor. Her cooking conditions weren't sanitary. And her business skills were lacking. She overcharged. She even cheated people by tipping her scales. So far, from everything we have learned, a lot of Delonda's accusations were nothing more than hearsay and gossip. She was lucky she didn't get sued."

Willow agreed. "I'd say."

Janie gasped. "You guys. I found another name on this list. You're not gonna believe who it is."

Just then the bell above the door chimed. Molly walked in and waved to Willow. She held up a piece of paper.

Willow waved. "I best go get the list she made for me for Saturday's cook-off. It's going to be interesting to see who all comes. I hope everyone does."

Janie grabbed her arm and showed her the name. Willow was confused. Molly? On Delonda's list? Then it dawned on her. Molly had told her about her café closing down. Molly was the little white woman Ms. Posey spoke of. The one who lost everything.

Willow dismissed the idea. Molly wouldn't hurt a fly. She was timid and allowed herself to be intimidated by people like Annabelle. She didn't have murder in her. No way.

Willow sat down opposite Molly. "You made the list. Thank you."

"I did. Sugar, I'm still not sure this is such a great idea." Molly was still questioning whether or not having the cook-off was too soon.

"I think it's going to go great. We could open up my shop and sell tickets to the town people. We could still make up some of that investment you lost out on."

Molly's eyes lit up. "Really? You'd be willing to do that? For me?"

"I don't see why not. We have the space. People can mill about outside and eat their chili. There is a few picnic tables outside and we can set up some banquet tables for more seating and there's the park across the street. I would think it would work, don't you?"

"Yes, I do believe it would. I'll call the newspaper and see if they'll run this in tomorrow's edition. And Stu down at the radio station might make an announcement for us on his radio program."

Willow smiled. This was the first time all week she had seen Molly with a smile on her face. She was happy she could be a part of that. She was such a sweet woman. Willow wondered how old she was. *She has to be at least 50.*

Molly stood to go and gave Willow a hug. "Sugar, I got to thank you! It has been a long time since anyone has done something this nice for me. I'm ever so grateful."

"You're welcome, Molly. It really is my pleasure."

Molly left with a little more spring in her step. Which in turn, gave Willow a bit of a bounce.

Steve, Embry, and Janie were waiting to see what Molly had to say and see who was on Molly's list. Almost everyone on Molly's list was also on Delonda's. Thankfully, Willow didn't see her own name on the "out to get you" list. If Delonda was still living, Willow had no doubt her name would have been handwritten on that list the very night of the cook-off. She sighed a breath of relief. Her little ice cream shop was safe from the wicked witch of the west.

Chapter 10

Willow unlocked her door then sat on the porch while Clover ran and did her thing. Thankfully she ran to the field to go potty. If she kept that up, Willow wouldn't have to clean up after her. That was the one job, well, that and hair removal, were the two things that Willow hated about having a dog. Everything else she loved. She had to admit, she was grateful to Steve for taking her to get Clover. She already loved her adopted daughter.

She lit a fire and started to look through her grandmother's recipes. What should she make for Steve? Was she really going to make something that she had yet to try? She doubted it. She pulled out her recipe for her favorite pot roast. That sounded so good. Add some mashed potatoes and gravy, maybe some honey glazed carrots, some homemade biscuits and she would have him eating out of her hands. She sighed. She'd be seeing that dimple all evening long. The thought brought a smile to her face. She liked him. She really did. And it would appear he might like her too.

Willow leaned back against the couch, notebook in hand, looking at the evidence. She was missing something. The list of suspects could be endless. Now that she had been cleared, the thought crossed her mind to just let Steve do his job and find the person responsible. Unfortunately, she couldn't quite shake the thoughts rolling through her mind. She couldn't put her finger on it. Not yet. But she would. Her gut had yet to fail her. Some might call it intuition. Some called it psychic ability. She had been told God gave people gifts. Perhaps this was hers. She just knew that she knew. Something wasn't right. She had a feeling everything would fall into place soon. Maybe Saturday. At least they would be one step closer to finding out who killed Delonda Posey.

She read the names to herself and repeated what she knew about each of her suspects thus far. First, the victim. If you could call her that. Some might say the murderer did the world a favor. Still, murder wasn't the answer. Delonda was a person no one wanted to be around. No one. It would seem, from her short conversation with her, that her own mother didn't enjoy her company or think too highly of her. She lived to destroy people. Who does that? Who is so unhappy they want everyone else around them to be miserable? Something had to of contributed to this person that Delonda had become. But what? What started her journey down this path? Or was she a born psychopath who just loved to destroy people?

Maybe if Willow understood the victim she would better understand the person who murdered her.

Now, for her suspects. Number one in her book was Richard Sutton, the judge whose barbecue sauce recipe was called on the carpet for being stolen. He was obviously prone to physical violence. Instead of just denying the accusation and banning her from his restaurant, he nearly came to blows with her. And would have if not for his employees keeping him at bay. Then why did he try to perform CPR when she collapsed in the bowl of chili? To put on a good show? To distract everyone and make them think he was her friend and not her murderer? So many questions. So few answers.

And what about Beau Lovett? He lost a lot of money because of her. His dream of opening a restaurant was put on hold, possibly forever, because this woman refused to play nice and compromise. Perhaps his only path of retribution was revenge. Did she push him over the top and turn a normally sane, rational man into a murderer? Could she affect someone that much?

Annabelle was the anomaly. She never mentioned, not once, her candy business being taken down. Knowing Annabelle, she didn't take that well. She may hide behind her Southern lady like manners but behind that façade was a woman who is used to getting what she wants. And when what she wants is taken away, well, the results wouldn't be pretty. Annabelle was smart enough to plot her revenge well. She would have taken her time and thought everything out.

She continued to look through the rest of the names, trying to make connections and see the unseen. Time would tell. The party was three days away and she had a ton to do. She set the list of suspects aside and started a new to do list. Cleaning, cleaning, and more cleaning.

Chapter 11

Willow had to run to the city for her ingredients for chili. She cleaned until her house shone and felt like it was time for a break. She tucked Clover away in her new Kennel then set off for the city. She had a list of ingredients to get, as well as a few things for the house. By the time she actually left it was getting late and she still hadn't eaten dinner yet. She called Embry.

"You hungry?"

"I could use a bite. You coming in to town?"

"Yeah, I gotta get some ingredients for my chili."

"Want to meet at Applebees?"

"Sounds good to me."

A half hour later Willow found herself sitting in a booth at the chain restaurant. Embry walked in a couple of minutes later. "You beat me. You actually drove the speed limit today?"

"I can drive the speed limit. That has never been the issue. I just don't like to."

Embry grinned. She loved giving her mom a hard time. Someone had to do it.

Both women glanced over their menus. Willow ordered a southwest chicken wrap and a bowl of French onion soup. Embry had the four cheese mac and cheese with bacon and chicken.

"How was dinner with the chief?" Embry asked.

"It didn't happen. He had an emergency at work." She shrugged her shoulders. Maybe next time.

"Anything new with the case? Did he find prints on the bag?"

Willow tapped her forehead. "I forgot to tell you. No, nothing. He found a big fat zero."

"Then we're right back where we started. Square one!"

Willow couldn't exactly disagree. She refused to give up. People didn't go around murdering people. Even if they deserved it. "We can't give up. The clues are out there. We just have to find them."

Willow agreed with her mom then changed the subject. "Want me to go to the store with you?" She took a bite of her pasta.

"Sure, you can keep me company."

"How is the shop doing? Better after the town figured out you weren't the murderer?"

"Much. We can hardly keep up. I took today off to get ready for Saturday. Janie and our part timer covered today. I have to make the chili tomorrow so it'll be ready and I completely spaced out I had run out of a few things. Tomorrow I'm working the shop so this was my only chance to get into town. I figured I could take a little time to come and see my favorite daughter."

"Only daughter, Mom."

"Well, I could adopt another if you fall out of my good graces."

Embry cast a wry look her way and took the last bite of her pasta. "That was good. Thanks for inviting me."

"You're welcome. I'm glad you could come. I'm going to run to the bathroom. I'll be right back."

"Mom?"

"Yeah?"

"Why don't you walk?"

"Oh hush."

Embry noticed her mother left her purse sitting on the seat. She always did that. She started laughing. She had to learn somehow. She slipped a little device in her purse for later.

Willow led the way into the grocery store. She was looking at labels on canned tomatoes when the guy next to her let a very loud noise escape from his derriere. Willow gave him a dirty look and moved down a little ways. *That was rude.* He seemed to be looking at her in the same manner.

She shook her head and put her items in her cart and moved on. "Did you hear the guy next to me? I had to get out of there. That was gross."

Embry agreed. It was gross. She smiled to herself.

Next they found themselves looking at chili powder and chipotle seasoning. This time some older lady next to Willow allowed some gas to pass. Willow was incredulous. The lady gave Willow a dirty look and left the aisle. "What is wrong with people tonight? And why are they looking at me like that?"

"I don't know, Mom. I think you just have that effect on people."

"Huh. That is just too weird. I wonder if something is in the air tonight. That lady really sounded like she needed to find a bathroom, and fast."

Embry almost lost it.

Willow had almost everything on her list. The last stop was the meat aisle. She needed her ground chuck and andouille sausage. She was picking up a package of meat when an old guy let one rip. "Seriously? What is up with you people tonight?"

"Lady, exactly what do you mean by you people? And that didn't come from me. That was you."

"People with gas problems, that's who. They're all over this store. And what do you mean that wasn't you? It most certainly wasn't me."

"It sure was. If I was you I'd go see your doctor. You don't know something like that is coming out of your body, you need a doctor. Trust me."

He took off.

Embry was laughing so hard she about peed her pants. "Oh, Mom. You are such an easy target." She reached in Willow's purse and pulled out the little device she'd planted earlier. Then she pressed the button on her remote and let a big one rip.

"You. This was you? I can't believe you. So everyone thought I was doing that?"

Embry was still laughing so hard she wasn't able to speak. She just nodded her head up and down.

"I'm going to get you back for this, you know that, right?"

"Mom, you needed to relax a little bit. This murder business has you in knots. Besides, you've got to quit leaving your purse lying around. Someone could take it or put something much worse in there. And with your luck, it could put you right back in the middle of a murder investigation. I know you don't want that!"

Chapter 12

The day of the chili cook-off was a gloriously sunny day. Willow was thankful. It meant more of the crowd would be willing to mill around outside and she wouldn't have to cram everyone in her house. The fact that both Beau and Richard were still willing to judge was something of a miracle to Willow. After the last attempt to hold the contest and the murder of Delonda, she was fairly certain judges were going to be hard to come by.

She was glad she was only having the entrants, judges, and a few helpers out at the house. The real party where the public was invited was to be held outside her shop and in the park across the street. The facilities were more appropriate in town but the house was more intimate for finding a murderer. Or at least to collect clues.

Embry and Janie had come early to help with all the last minute preparations. Willow had made her chili the night before and had it simmering on her new stove. She was able to switch to gas and loved the difference it made in her cooking. She took a bite of her chili and smiled. Delicious. Clover was bouncing around anticipating the arrival of all the guests. She knew something was up and her energy level was clearly elevated.

Molly was the first of the guests to arrive. Willow helped her get set up.

Willow eyed the trophy sitting on the counter. She took it and placed it on the mantle above the fire place, just to see what it would look like.

Steve found her admiring it. "You counting on keeping that there?"

She grabbed the trophy and placed it back on the counter. "I was just seeing how it would look." She looked around. "I hope no one else saw me."

"I wouldn't worry about it. Everyone who entered this contest has their eye on that trophy. You aren't the only one." He gave her hand a squeeze. "Where is Clover?"

She's outside with Embry and Janie. Hopefully she doesn't get into too much trouble. I should put her in her kennel soon or she'll be tempted to taste the chili. She could be the third judge."

"She would like that. I'm not sure anyone else would though. Especially not the cooks who made the food."

Willow put Clover in her kennel and secured her. She went outside to see how everyone was doing in finding their places. She was enjoying playing hostess. She looked around for Molly and couldn't find her anywhere. A few minutes later Willow saw her walk out the front door. She looked around, as if checking to see if anyone noticed. Thinking she was in the clear, she headed toward Annabelle who had just arrived.

That is strange.

The chili stations were filling up. It looked like everyone came. Janie had been right. The killer wouldn't have wanted to be a no show. Everyone would have noticed.

Embry and Janie were milling around listening to conversations and basically collecting anything they found helpful. Steve came as her date and not as the police chief. Knowing this helped some of the entrants to lower their guard. They somehow forgot there was a killer on the loose. Even if it was most likely one of them.

Willow wanted to talk with Beau and Richard, separately and looked for an opportunity to do so. The first person she came across on her list was Annabelle. She wasn't sure she was ready for Annabelle, but, opportunity knocked so she answered.

"Hey, Annabelle. I see you made it."

Annabelle looked at Willow as if she were an alien. "Of course I made it. I want that trophy." She set her pot down at her station. "I paid my entry fee and I'm here to win."

"So, is your secret ingredient chocolate?" Willow wasn't sure what to expect but the glare she received in response to her question spoke volumes.

"No, I no longer work with chocolate." Annabelle deposited her chili in her chafing dish while she spoke. "Who told you I used to make chocolates? And no, I didn't kill the woman. Even if I did think she was the coldest, nastiest woman on the face of the earth. Who treats people that way? She was downright mean." She sniffled a little. "I always dreamed of having my own chocolate shop. She took that away from me." She looked a little guilty. "I hate to say it, but I'm kind of glad she is dead. She wasn't a nice person."

Willow walked away with a little bit more compassion for Annabelle. They may never see eye to eye on a lot of things, but Annabelle was truly affected by Delonda's cruel treatment. She was human and perhaps just a bit more fragile than she let on. Perhaps her tough Southern lady routine was simply a way for her to feel better about herself. She found a way to cope. Almost like armor to protect herself with. Which then begged the question: since Annabelle is so good at hiding her true feelings, is she also good at hiding murder?

Willow walked around looking for her next suspect. Beau Lovett was just coming out of the house. She caught up with him and outstretched her hand. "Hi, I don't think we met. I'm Willow. This is my place."

He shook her hand. "I'm Beau. But you already know that."

She struggled to keep up as he strode across the yard. He was at least 6'5". "Yes, I do know who you are. I'm sorry if I implied otherwise. I just wanted to formally meet."

"No problem. We've met. Thanks for hosting the re-schedule."

He started to walk away from her when she asked him straight out, "Beau, how much money did you lose because of Delonda?"

He stopped and spun around. "None of your business. And no, I did not kill that vile woman. Not that it didn't cross my mind. But that is not how I operate. I would have destroyed her at her own game had she stuck around long enough. I didn't have to kill her body. Her soul would have been enough for me." He turned around and stomped to the judges table. Boy, she was glad he wouldn't know which pot of chili was hers!

Kill her soul? What did he mean by that? She would have to bring that up to Embry and Janie. Perhaps they heard something today to add to his comment.

She looked around for Richard. *He has to be here somewhere.* She finally spotted him talking with Embry. Hopefully she was getting some good information from him. Molly was calling the judging to order. She would have to corner him after the trophy was awarded.

Willow realized she hadn't seen Steve in a while. *Where did he go? Some date he is!* She shook her head. It was so hard to keep up with everyone. She was supposed to be solving a murder case, not a missing person's case. She took her spot next to her chili. She was still a contestant and she still wanted to win. Even if she was trying to solve a murder.

The judges finally finished tasting all the chili. Richard and Beau were joined by a newcomer Molly recruited; Steve. How did he get roped into this?

She double checked her number. This time her chili was number 11.

Molly took the stage. "Okay everybody, listen up. I have the judges' decisions on the winners. The second runner up is Mitch Roberts."

Everyone clapped.

He never made the "list" so Willow hadn't taken any real interest in him.

Molly continued. "The first runner up is number 17. Miss Annabelle Josephine Butterfield."

Willow watched Annabelle bounce up to the stage and accept her trophy. Her blond curls bouncing the entire way up the stairs. Of course she had to thank everyone and she literally thanked everyone from her mother and father to her pastor at church. The woman had a lot of thanks, that much was for sure. She carried her trophy back to her station and gave Willow a little stare.

"Now ya'll, for the grand prize winner. Number 11, Miss Willow Crier."

Willow let out a yelp. "I won? Really?" She ran up the stage completely forgetting about her little tirade of jealousy a moment before. She won! "Oh Molly, I won. I won." She briefly thought about sticking her tongue out at Annabelle then reconsidered. She would be the grown up.

Chapter 13

Embry waited until her mother had the trophy in her hand before screaming for help. They had planned a diversion so her mom and Janie could quickly search the entrants' stations. It was the only solution they came up with to be able to physically search the work stations.

The screaming started as soon as Willow stepped off the stage.

Everyone ran for Embry, who was obviously upset and in need of help. She'd been playing with Clover and her diamond engagement ring had fallen off. She was in tears. Everyone was down on their hands and knees, crawling around on the ground searching for the missing diamond. Willow just shook her head. They would never find it because there wasn't one. None the less, Willow and Janie started running from station to station, hoping to find something. Anything.

Steve started for Embry then caught sight of Willow and Janie. He joined the two women. "What do you think you two are doing?"

Willow didn't have time to stop and talk. "What does it look like? Go look at Annabelle's station then see if you can find Molly's purse."

The chief stood still. "Willow, I cannot be illegally searching anyone's things. I think I'll go look for the engagement ring and leave the snooping to you and Janie."

She didn't even take the time for eye contact. "Suit yourself." Then she ran to Annabelle's station. She figured they each had about ten minutes to find something before the search party became wary and wandered back to load their chili and take it to the park. She had a lot of ground to cover and not enough time to do a thorough job. Something was better than nothing. From Annabelle's station she moved to Beau's.

Somehow Beau had left his phone behind. She took a cursory glance at the screen and recognized a number. Who do I know that he would be texting? She read the portion of the message that was visible. She committed the number to memory so she could look in her phone for the same number. She replaced the phone then moved on. It was the only clue she found.

Janie found a big fat zip. Nothing.

***

Steve helped Willow load up her chili into his truck then drove the short distance into town while she was searching her phone for recognizable numbers. She knew that number in Beau's phone. She was sure of it.

"Ah ha! There it is." She looked at the chief. "Do you know how Molly and Beau Lovett know one another? He has a text message from her on his phone. I could only read the little bit that was on the front notices, but it was definitely from her. And she asked him if he found it."

Steve looked at her as he was parking. "Found what?"

She shrugged her shoulders. "I have no idea. But she certainly wanted to know." She thought back to the cook off. "You know what? Earlier tonight, I saw Molly come out of the house looking guilty about something then a few minutes later I saw Beau do the same thing. I wonder what is up with those two."

People were already mingling in the park. It seemed as if the whole town came out to support the cook-off. Or maybe it was just an excuse to get out of cooking for the evening. Either way, Willow was just thankful for the support. A week ago she was wondering if she would have to leave town with her tail between her legs. Now, it seemed she was in the town's good graces again. People had been buying tickets all week for the chili dinner.

Molly was thrilled. She had taken a hit for the cook off expenses and wasn't able to recoup her investment. This was putting her back in the black.

Even Cookie had shown up and helped out. She had big pans of cornbread to accompany the chili. Willow's part timers had chopped enough onions and dished up enough grated cheese and sour cream for everyone to top off their bowls as they saw fit. Willow had opened her shop and offered a discount on ice cream cones for dessert. Someone had set up a temporary stage and a local band was playing country music. The night couldn't have been more perfect. Well, it could have. If Willow had found the murderer. That would have made the evening perfect.

She sidled up to Molly who had just taken a long sip of sweet tea. "How are you? I've hardly got to say two words to you all evening."

Molly jumped. "Goodness, you scared me. Do you always sneak up on people like that?" She regained her composure. "Happy as a dead pig in the sunshine. Turns out this idea of yours was a sure thing. Thank you. You saved my hide."

Why in the world would a dead pig be happy in the sunshine? "Um, okay. You're welcome then." Willow was quiet for a moment. "I'm not sure people really came out to commemorate Delonda, but that's okay. We had fun anyway."

"I think you're right. Most people who knew her didn't really like her at all." Molly looked around. "I invited her mother but I guess she had better things to do. She didn't show up. I'm fixin' to give her a call later. Tell her we missed her. Bless her little heart."

"Yes, if Delonda's own mother wasn't interested in honoring her child, I guess there wouldn't be too many other people who cared either. Which is just sad. Everyone should have someone who cares about them." Willow skillfully changed the subject, or so she thought. "Was that you and Beau I saw leaving together earlier out at the ranch?"

Molly stumbled over her words. "Me and Beau? Together? Oh, Honey, no. You must be mistaken."

"Oh, for some reason I thought I saw you two together. Must have been someone else."

Willow watched Molly excuse herself for the restroom. Molly pulled out her phone as she was walking. Willow wished she could see who she was texting. But she had a pretty good guess.

As Willow was turning to the ice cream shop, she noticed a lone figure standing off by himself. A tall, dark, handsome man who seemed to be watching the major players in the suspect pool.

Chapter 14

The next day Willow caught up with Richard Sutton. He had skipped the chili dinner in the park, saying he was needed at his restaurant. Whether or not he was telling the truth, she didn't know. He'd made his appearance. If he was the killer, then he didn't consider leaving early a statement of guilt.

She decided she was in the mood for some real southern barbecue. She drug Embry along for good measure. "Let's watch Mr. Sutton in action, shall we?"

Willow didn't want to make Richard mad. She had already seen what he was capable of. She didn't want to be banned either, especially if the barbecue was as good as it was rumored to be. She ordered a pulled pork barbecue sandwich and an order of sweet potato fries. Embry decided to try their barbecue chicken and garlic mashed potatoes. Both were delicious.

Richard Sutton was a genius as far as Willow was concerned. The stuff she was rolling around on her tongue could have been the best barbecue she had ever eaten. She'd had some good barbecue in her day. She could understand why he was so upset with Delonda and her accusations. He passed by their table and she called out to him.

"Mr. Sutton. Hi, it's me, Willow, from the chili cook-off."

He seemed a bit distracted and looked nervously toward the door. He said hi just as the door opened and Beau and Molly walked in the door. At first the pair smiled and waved at Richard, until Richard pointed out Willow, then their demeanor changed. Especially Molly's.

Molly turned seven shades of red and immediately backed out of the front door, her eyes never leaving Willow's.

Willow turned to Embry. "Things are about to get interesting."

Beau marched over to her table. "What are you doing here?" He demanded.

"I heard Richard's barbecue was the best around and I just had to see for myself." She wiped her mouth with her napkin. "I also know something fishy is going on with you—three." She thought it was only Beau and Molly, but now, she was certain Richard had his hand in whatever was going on as well. But what? Did they all three plot Delonda's murder together?

Beau stormed out of the restaurant. Willow presumed after Molly. He probably wanted to make sure she didn't do anything stupid, like confess. Willow shook her head. She had really liked Molly. What had she been thinking? And then to lie on top of it all. Molly really should reconsider attending Bible study. Or maybe not. Bible study was probably the best place for murderers and liars.

Just as Willow was turning back to her sandwich, she noticed the same man seated near her who had been quietly observing at last night's chili in the park. It was no coincidence, of that she was sure. She had to find out who he was. She stood up as if to go the restroom then turned and seated herself at his table.

"Who are you?" She demanded without introducing herself.

She should have given Embry a heads up, but decided to just go for it. Her daughter would probably have tried to talk her out of it.

The young man looked to be around 30. He had dark, ebony skin and a large hands with delicate long fingers. She would guess a piano player. She waited for his answer.

"Why do you want to know?"

"Because I saw you out at the chili picnic and now here you are at the restaurant of one of the judges. I think you're up to something."

He nodded. "I've been watching you too. I have the same goal in mind, to find out who murdered my girlfriend."

Willow's mouth dropped open. "Delonda was your girlfriend?"

"Yes, she was."

Willow started to react then remembered he was probably grieving. At least she hoped he was. She would hate to add another suspect to her already mind numbing list. "I'm sorry for your loss." He genuinely looked upset. She was relieved.

He nodded, accepting her condolences.

Then she continued. "Do you have any leads? Any information to help us catch a murderer?"

"I only know what Delonda told me. Someone had been threatening her, leaving messages on her cell phone, sending her threats at the newspaper. But, that stuff had been happening for a long time." He shook his head in doubt. "I don't think it's the same person. No, I think the murderer is someone entirely different."

She happened to agree with him. She already knew of the threats, of which there had been many. Steve had filled her in on those. No, this was someone who was taking their revenge to another level altogether.

He ran his hand over his barely there hair. "I know Delonda was a difficult person. I know she had made more enemies than most people put together. But that was her persona. That was who she was in public. It was part of her branding, as she liked to call it. In private she was caring and loving."

Willow highly doubted the lovey dovey bit, but, hey, the guy was obviously living in a dream world. Even her mother saw Delonda for who she was, a manipulative, conniving, self-serving, woman who would step on anyone and anything to get what she wanted. Willow figured someone finally got sick of her antics and put a stop to it. This person was a doer. A person who followed through. Not someone who made idle threats.

"I'm Willow, by the way." She finally decided to use some manners and introduce herself.

"I know who you are." He extended his hand. "I'm Tayven."

Willow shook his hand, very carefully. She didn't want to hurt those piano hands. If he didn't play piano, he should.

Tayven was still talking. She hoped she didn't miss anything.

"Like I said, I've been trying to figure this thing out. I'm at a dead end. I just don't know if the person who did this is ever going to pay for what they did."

"We're going to find them. Is there anything at all, anything you can think of, even something that doesn't seem to make a difference in the grand scheme of things? Anything Delonda told you or might have hinted at?"

"You know, she kept talking about this one woman from years back. When she first got started on her column and before she started her vlog, about how this one woman was out to get her. She never did tell me her name. I wish she had. But, the thing is, she swore the woman had tried to kill her once before, by using peanuts in her baked goods. I think it's too much of a coincidence now that the killer actually used peanuts to murder her. Delonda didn't let too many people know about her allergy. In fact, if she hadn't of had a mild reaction the morning of the cook-off, to the medications she was on, she probably would have lived. The medical examiner said the two combined just went into over drive and her body wouldn't have recovered, even if she had recognized the signs and used her EpiPen."

He swallowed a large gulp of tea. "I don't understand why she didn't even try. People said she didn't even go for her epi. Why didn't she? She knows when she is having an allergic reaction."

Willow wished she had answers for him. And she hoped to soon. But, at the moment, she didn't. All she could do is pat his hand and comfort him best she knew how. While doing so, her mind was stuck on the lady who had used peanuts to made Delonda sick once before. Who was she? She had to get to the bottom of this. She just had to.

Willow exchanged phone numbers with Tayven and promised to let him know if she figured anything out. He promised to call her if he thought of anything that might shed some light on who wanted his girlfriend dead.

Chapter 15

Willow dropped Embry off then headed to the shop. She had to play catch up. This murder business was keeping her from her tasks. She had to practice better time management skills. She tucked her phone in her pocket. No distractions. None.

She made three batches each of her banana bread and her world famous cinnamon rolls. Okay, they weren't world famous. Yet. But, they were Turtle famous. She patted her thighs. She would know. She spoke to the gooey dough before her. "I have a love hate relationship with you, you know that, right?" Her mind drifted to the cinnamon treat and knew she'd be having one, or possibly two, of those for supper. If she got them finished.

Her phone buzzed in her pocket. She ignored it. She had to take care of business. A few minutes later, she heard pounding on the shop door. She washed her hands then went to the door. She opened the door to Molly, who was drenched in either tears or snot, or perhaps both.

"Molly, come in. I'm surprised to see you here."

"I'm sorry, Willow. I really am. I've been a fool and I've got to get some things off my chest." She blubbered some more.

Willow waited. She assured Molly that confession was good for the soul then sat down to hear her out.

"I know I've been acting kind of crazy lately." She blew her nose on a cloth handkerchief. She wrung her hands together. "I'm nervous as a long-tail cat in a room full of rocking chairs."

Willow shuddered. Cloth? What happened to good old fashioned tissues? And what in the world does any of this have to do with cats and rocking chairs?

"I just didn't know who I could talk to."

"You've come to the right person. You can talk to me." Willow listened intently as Molly began to tell the whole sordid story. She could just imagine the bitterness at having your café, your livelihood taken away from you by a woman on a mission. She even understood Molly wanting revenge…

"Willow, are you listening to me?" She dabbed her nose.

Willow shook her head. "Yes, I was listening. You said you killed Delonda because she took your café away, because she placed your entire family in financial devastation, because she ruined you.

"No, I didn't say that. You weren't listening."

What? She didn't confess? Willow leaned forward in her chair. "Didn't you come here to confess? I thought you needed someone to talk to?"

"Yes, I did come to confess…

Willow cut her off. "See, I was listening."

"No, you weren't. I didn't come here to confess to murdering no one. I came to confess something altogether different. I lied to you the other night. I was with Beau in your house."

Willow watched the waterworks start again. Who cares whether or not she was in the house if it doesn't have anything to do with Delonda's murder! "Spill it, Molly."

"I'm trying…I am. I'm such a horrible person. Beau and I are starting a café together. He is helping me get back on my feet, and get my good name restored."

Willow scrunched up her face. "That's it?"

"You thought I was going to confess to Delonda's murder? How could you think something like that?" Molly started crying all over again.

"You were slinking around. You were acting guilty."

"No, I was trying to be considerate. I didn't want people to think I was benefiting from her being gone. We thought it would be best to let things smooth over before we told anyone what we were up to. Richard is going in on it with us. And tonight, when you saw us, I knew I had to tell you. The guilt was eating me alive."

Did Willow hear that right? The guilt over keeping their business venture a secret was eating her alive? Who thinks that way? "So, are you saying you didn't kill Delonda Posey?"

"No, goodness, no. I would never kill anyone."

"You came here to confess that you're reopening your café? That's it?"

Molly sniffed. "Well, there is one other thing."

Willow perked up. "Ha! Tell me!"

"Beau and I started seeing each other, romantically that is. I just had to tell you. I'm so happy except when I'm trying to hide how I really feel. Now, I can be open and tell the world. I'm in love and I'm getting my business back."

Willow watched Molly turn from a babbling cry baby into a joyful woman in love. Willow gave

Molly a hug. "I'm so glad for you. You deserve to be happy."

Molly thanked her and told her she would keep her updated on the café's progress as well as her relationship with Beau. She was all smiles when she left.

Willow returned to her bread and cinnamon rolls. She had everything prepared for Janie for the next morning. She yawned and looked at her watch. She couldn't wait to cuddle up with Clover.

Chapter 16

Willow stepped up to her front porch and immediately heard Clover barking. She nearly had her key to the keyhole when she noticed the door was slightly ajar. She was certain she didn't leave it that way. She looked around and didn't see Embry's vehicle. Not that she would leave the door open. Nor would she forget to shut it if she had come out for something. At least Willow didn't think so.

She pulled out her phone and texted Steve. She didn't even know if Steve texted, but if the intruder was still in the house, she wanted to be as quiet as possible and perhaps catch them in the act. She pulled out her Taser then pushed the door farther open.

Clover was barking non-stop. She was kenneled but if she had been loose, they wouldn't have gotten in the door. She peeked around the corner. Nothing amiss in the living room area. She could see as far as the kitchen and there was no movement. She ventured farther into the house and tiptoed down the hall, listening for any out of place sounds. Nothing.

She opened the bedroom doors, one at a time. Still nothing. And nothing seemed out of place. She could rule out a robbery. Her television was still in place as was her laptop.

Willow checked her own room last. Bed was askew, but that was how she left it. She looked in her walk in closet, nothing messed up there. Next she checked her bathroom, just in case the person was hiding out waiting to attack. No one in sight. But, whoever it was had left a clear message on the bathroom mirror. "Stop. Or you're next!" She let Clover out of her kennel and the dog went crazy running around through the house, sniffing everything in sight.

Willow heard tires and saw headlights shine through her living room window. *Must be Steve.* She went to the front door and watched as he jogged to her front door.

"Are you okay? I tried to call you, but you didn't answer. You scared me to death."

"I'm fine."

"Why did you go in there? You should have waited for me."

"Clover was barking like a mad woman and I wanted to catch them in the act." She held up her Taser. "Besides, they would have been hurting if they had still been in here. I have to move getting my concealed carry up on my to-do list. Seriously."

"I take it they are long gone?"

Willow nodded her head and pet Clover. The dog rubbed her head against Willow's leg.

"Well, is anything missing?"

"Nope, not that I can tell."

"What did they want?" He looked around the open area. "Doesn't look too messed up in here. They weren't searching for hidden treasure."

She beckoned him to follow her. "Come on, I'll show you."

She allowed him to enter her bathroom and watched his reaction.

"Willow, you are making someone very uncomfortable." He called the office and two officers were on their way to gather finger prints and look for any evidence that might have been hiding.

Together they went to the kitchen and she started to heat up the cinnamon rolls she brought home. "Eat supper yet?"

"No, but I'd rather you not doing anything in here until my guys have a look around. Why don't you and Clover come with me? We'll grab a sandwich. Give my guys some time to work without three extra people underway." He went back to the bathroom. "Willow, I've never seen you wear lipstick. Is this written in yours?"

"Nope, it sure isn't. I'm a gloss kind of girl. That could only have come from the intruder. Who I'm also thinking is our murderer."

"Glad to know we're thinking alike."

Willow gathered up Clover's leash and a few treats and a couple plastic bags, just in case. She waited by Steve's truck as he led his officers through her house and showed them the message. It wasn't but a few minutes later Steve was opening her door for her and they were driving toward town.

Chapter 17

The next morning Willow's phone rang early. Earlier than she wanted to be getting up. She looked at the caller id. Janie. It would figure.

She put her on speaker. "What do you want?"

"Good morning to you too."

"What's so good about it?"

"Do you have your newspaper yet? There is something you're going to want to see on page nine."

Willow yawned. "And this something couldn't have waited an hour or two?"

"Willow, get up and get your paper."

"Okay, I'm up. Sheesh. I'll call you back in a little bit."

She brushed her teeth, let out the dog, and started the coffee pot before opening her newspaper. The older generation still received a paper. The younger generation got all their news from Yahoo. She was in the middle and did a little of both.

She unwrapped the cinnamon roll and put it in the microwave. While that was heating, she poured herself a cup of coffee, added a little cream, then sat down at the dinette set with her breakfast and the newspaper. Just as she turned the pages, the dog started barking to be let in.

Willow let Clover in and noticed she had something in her mouth. "Hey girl, what do you have there?" She took the item from the dog's mouth. It was a piece of cloth. A torn piece of cloth. Like someone had been running through the yard in the dark didn't see the bush and ended up in a tango. "Huh, I wonder who lost part of their pants." She examined the bright pink sweat material. It matched the lipstick on her mirror. "Who would wear bright pink to break into someone's house?"

She put the cloth in a zip up baggie and settled at the table with her coffee and cinnamon roll. She deeply breathed in the scent of cinnamon emanating from warm confection. The butter she spread on top was melting and oozing its way down into the layers. She put the roll to her lips and her phone rang, again. She closed her eyes and counted to three.

She answered with a slight attitude. "What?"

"Um, hi. Did I interrupt something?"

Steve. She sighed. "No, just trying to ingest five hundred calories of cinnamon goo and it's not going so well. Not for a lack of trying though, trust me." She sipped her coffee. Thank goodness that was acceptable phone etiquette.

"I just called to see how you're doing this morning, after last night's episode."

"Besides lacking my much needed eight hours, and being awoken from a particularly lovely dream, and since I'm going to have to reheat this cinnamon roll for the second time and it's going to be rubber by the time I get to it, I'm good. How are you?"

He chuckled. "You really aren't a morning person, are you?"

"And what gave you that idea?" She popped a piece of roll in her mouth and didn't care if she chewed in his ear. She was eating the darn cinnamon roll.

He just laughed. "Well, I guess I better get back to work."

She almost forgot to tell him about Clover's find. "Hey, Clover was out for her morning constitutional and came across some fabric caught in our bush out back. I'm thinking someone tried to cross my backyard in the dark and lost a little something from their pants. I put it in a storage baggie. I could bring it in to town when I go to the shop."

"I'm just around the corner from your house. Why don't I stop by and pick it up?"

"Okay, suit yourself. Coffee is on. You'll have to fight me for the cinnamon roll, though."

"See you in a few."

She finally opened the newspaper to page nine. There on the right hand side was a picture of Annabelle, the new food columnist, taking Delonda's place. Willow's mouth dropped. "You have got to be kidding me?"

Willow took her time reading through the article. Looked like Annabelle was trying to pick up where Delonda left off, with a review of a local eatery. It wasn't exactly scathing like Delonda's reviews, but it wasn't positive either. She had also included a recipe for her favorite chocolate caramel peanut bars. Just a sample of the recipes that were to come.

Willow shook her head. Molly was reopening her café. She and Beau were dating now. Richard was investing in the re-opening. And just because Molly said she didn't murder Delonda didn't mean she was innocent. Like a murderer would tell the truth. Then there was Annabelle, who not two weeks later already had an article in the paper taking Delonda's place as their resident food columnist. And just because pink was the intruder's color of choice didn't mean that neither Richard nor Beau was Delonda's killer. They weren't cleared yet. Not in Willow's book.

The knock at the window brought her to the present and she rose to answer. Clover was already barking. "What a good girl." Willow patted her head then opened the door for Steve. "Come on in."

He pet the dog then followed Willow back to the kitchen area.

She held up the paper. "Did you see this?"

He shook his head. "No, what is it?"

Willow showed him the article and told him about Molly's visit. In the aftermath of the prior evening's break in, she had forgotten to tell him about everything she learned. She ended up giving him the second cinnamon roll and sending him on his way. She had a hunch, and she had to do some research before she knew whether or not she was on the right track.

Chapter 18

Willow watched every vlog post Delonda ever put on her YouTube channel. Every. Single. One. That was a lot of Delonda. A lot more than Willow ever wanted to see. She went all the way back to the very first one.

When her phone rang, she answered it without looking at who was calling. "Did you get my message?"

She looked at the screen. The number had been blocked. "Who is this?"

Obviously the caller was trying to disguise their voice. It almost sounded like the horse whisperer on the other end. "Hello, did you say something? I can barely hear you?"

Again the caller spoke softly. "Did you get my message?"

"What? What did you say? You're going to have to speak up?" Willow was trying not to laugh. If the situation wasn't so serious she would have.

Finally the caller screamed. "Did you get my message?"

"Oh, it's you. I was wondering who was whispering in my phone. I'm getting older. The old hearing is going, ya know? Do you mean the message on my mirror? Yeah, I got it."

"Good. It would pay for you to heed the message. Stop snooping. Or you're next."

The click on the other end signified the caller had ended their conversation. She set her cell phone down. *The murderer has my personal phone number?* Now things were starting to become clear. Willow had a bit of a road trip to take. She called Janie at the shop. "Can you handle things for a little bit? I need to run an errand."

"Yeah, sure. Thanks for getting the bread and rolls done last night."

"No problem. I know I've been pre-occupied and I really appreciate all the time you've been putting in at the shop."

"Hey, what's more important? Catching a murderer or baking a few pans of brownies? Oh, and I have to tell you Cookie stopped in the shop this morning. She said she is going to have to resign from her baking duties. She is going to be helping Molly out at the café and won't have time to do both. Not with working the lunch periods at the high school.

"Okay, we'll figure it out. I'm sure my focus will be where it needs to be soon. I can probably pick up the extra slack or we can find someone else who might be interested."

Willow needed to think. She needed to set everything aside and just get into her own mind. She grabbed a bottle of water and set off on foot. Exercise wouldn't hurt either. She always thought best on her feet.

One by one she went over each suspect. She thought about all the vlog posts she had seen and then it hit her. There was one post she didn't see. One person whose business she knew had been affected by Delonda, who openly admitted to the fact, whose whole fall from grace wasn't there for the world to see. Why not? She turned and jogged for home. She was out of breath by the time she reached her house. She hadn't realized she had gone so far. She put Clover on her leash and brought her along for the ride. It might be best to have the dog with her anyhow. For protection and all that. Then she patted her purse which held her handy Taser.

Her first stop was Delonda's mother's house.

She knocked on the door.

"Oh, it's you again." She pushed open the screen door then turned and walked in the living room, once again expecting Willow to follow.

Willow sat down on the indicated chair then bulldozed straight ahead. "Ms. Posey, do you happen to know an Annabelle Josephine Butterfield?"

"Why, I sure do. That little girl grew up right next door to us when we lived down on the bad side of town. Course, her name wasn't all that fancy back then. Just Ann Baker. She went and changed her name when she got all uppity and dropped my little girl as a best friend like a hot potato just come out of the microwave." She lifted her tea mug to her lips. "I see she done took over my girl's column in the paper. I didn't know for sure it was her until I saw her picture, but yeah, that's Ann Baker. Little white girl growing up next door to us. Her mama and daddy were mean drunks. She always fantasized about being a southern belle. She ain't no southern belle. If she is, then I'm white."

Ms. Posey laughed at her own joke and slapped her leg. "I just keep getting funnier and funnier in my old age. I swear I do." She sobered up. "You think Ann is the one who killed Delonda? They used to be real good friends. Real good. It hurt Delonda bad when Ann decided she was too good for the likes of Delonda. Mmhmm. It sure did. After that I lost track of the girl.

Course, I didn't know she went and changed her name."

"Ms. Posey, do you remember what they fought about?"

"Oh girl, I forgot all about that. Now that you mention it, I do remember. Delonda accused Ann of trying to kill her. She gave her some chocolate she made and put peanuts in it. Ann knew Delonda was deathly allergic to peanuts. She didn't care. Delonda had started to make a name for herself and Ann was jealous. She had always been a jealous girl. And so full of herself. She thought the sun and moon rose because of her. Full of herself, I say." She swallowed hard. "My girl didn't do much better. But I don't think she up and killed nobody. She did ruin quite a few people's lives though. She said it did them good. Leveled out the playing field, so to speak. All those restaurant owners who never had to work hard for what they got. I tried to tell her, not everybody's rich. And not all rich people think they're God's gift to the world. But she wouldn't listen. That girl was hard headed. Had to do things her way. Her way got her killed."

"Oh, Ms. Posey. I wish you would have come to the commemorative chili cook-off, I really wish you had. You could have revealed

Annabelle's true identity and we'd be finished with all of this ugly business."

"Honey, I wasn't gonna go to some dinner where everyone attending was glad she was gone. I didn't even like her sometimes, but she was my baby and I loved her. I wasn't ready to be around that kind of crowd."

Willow told her once again how sorry she was then said goodbye. She called Steve from the phone and told him to meet her at Annabelle's.

Chapter 19

Willow's phone buzzed. She peeked. It was Steve. She decided it was best not to answer. He left a voice mail then he texted. "Wait for me. Do not go by yourself. I repeat, wait for me."

She patted Clover's head. "I'm not by myself, am I girl?" She ignored the text. What if she takes off? What if she's on her way out of town and we miss her? I can't wait. Besides, Steve will be there soon enough. She can't do too much damage before he gets there.

Willow pulled up in front of the two story home. Annabelle had sure found a way to pull off the whole southern belle part. The house was located on the outside edges of the big city, nearly to Turtle. She even had the house with the white pillars going on. Willow shook her head. "I'd rather be a Yankee then pretend I'm something I'm not."

She watched the house for any sign of movement. Annabelle's car was parked in the driveway. Willow patted her purse, thankful for her Taser. A gun would have been better but, she had to make do with what she had. Besides, if she shot the woman it might not look too good. Willow opened her car door just as the front door to Annabelle's house opened. Annabelle was pulling a suitcase behind her.

"Ah ha!" Willow got out and waved to her, hoping she looked friendly and not accusatory. "Annabelle, hi, I was in the neighborhood and thought I'd stop by and say, hi." Even to Willow's ears the excuse sounded lame. Why didn't she practice something better than that? Her phone buzzed in her pocket. Once again, she ignored it. She bounced up the walk.

"You going on a trip?"

Annabelle's eyes darted up and down the street. "Yeah, my mama is sick so I'm going to Savannah to spend some time with her. Just until she gets better."

Willow nearly rolled her eyes at the lie but caught herself. "I'm so sorry. I hope she's gonna be okay."

"I'm sure she'll be right as rain. We southern women are made of sturdy stock. She won't be down long." She cocked her head as if in thought. "So, what are you doing in my neighborhood anyway?"

As soon as she asked the question Willow heard Clover barking. She had left her window down far enough the dog could get out, just in case Annabelle pulled something crazy and Willow needed Clover's help. What she didn't count on was Clover remembering Annabelle from the break in.

Clover was standing next to Willow with her fur raised and her teeth bared. Willow was trying to get her to settle down so she wouldn't blow her cover. She should have known Annabelle would figure it out.

"So, what gave me away?"

Willow stayed next to Clover's side. "A few things. One, you said Delonda had caused your candy business to fail. Yet, there wasn't one vlog post about you on her YouTube station. Either she didn't have a hand in your candy business failing, you never had a candy business, or there was something else entirely between the two of you. I chose the latter. Next, did you really mean to write in your own lipstick on my mirror? The only person I know who wears that bright of lipstick is you. Then, you ripped your bright pink sweatpants when you got tangled up in my bush in my backyard. Who wears hot pink when they break into someone's house? Anyone else would have worn black. Your fatal mistake though was taking over Delonda's column so soon. You didn't count on Ms. Posey recognizing you for who you really are—Ann Baker. Not Annabelle Josephine Butterfield, from that Butterfield family. No, you grew up on the other side of the tracks and you completely fabricated a whole new identity for yourself. You played the part of the refined Southern Lady, the Southern Belle. Did I get it right?"

Before Willow knew what was happening, Annabelle—Ann—or whoever she claimed to be—was holding a small gun pointed right at Clover. "Shut the dog up or you both will die."

Willow moved her hand toward her purse and realized she left it on the front seat of the car. *Willow, your daughter warned you about leaving your purse places!* Willow wanted to get Annabelle's mind off the dog and tried to distract her. "Well, you didn't tell me if I got it right."

Annabelle smirked. "Close enough. Enough that you can't stick around to talk about it, that's for sure. Did Ms. Posey tell you that Delonda never let me forget who I really was? Did she tell you that Delonda was always whispering in my ear how she could ruin everything for me? How if I didn't give her what she wanted and if I didn't help her get the dirt on who she wanted to take down that she would threaten to expose me? Did she tell you that? I'm not a mean person. I'm not out to hurt people like she did. I just didn't want to be poor Ann Baker anymore. I wanted to be someone who mattered, someone who had a history and a past they could be proud of. She ruined everything. Or she almost did." She shook her head. "I can't let you do the same thing. I won't let you. I've worked too hard to get where I am. Nobody is going to expose me, especially not a Yankee." She motioned with her gun hand to walk toward the house.

As soon as Willow started walking, Clover dove for her hand and the gun went off. Clover whimpered yet still hung on to Annabelle's wrist. Annabelle was thrashing around.

Willow dove for the gun just as Steve pulled up and jumped out of his car. "I told you to wait!" He pulled his revolver on Annabelle who was still on the ground. Several city police cars pulled up right after he did.

Willow cradled Clover in her arms and cried.

Steve yelled to one of the officers. "Get that dog to the vet. We've got this situation under control."

The officer picked up Clover and Willow ran behind him. Together they drove with the lights on to the nearest vet. She was immediately taken back to surgery. Willow hung out in the waiting room, the blood on her shirt reminding her of her heroine. She paced back and forth as she waited.

Embry ran into the veterinarian's waiting room and gathered her mom in a huge hug. "Oh. Mom, is she okay?"

"I don't know yet, honey. I'm hoping to hear something soon."

Steve came through the door. "I had to come find out how you are. Annabelle, or Ann, whatever, is in custody. I have to get back but I was hoping there would be some word about Clover."

As soon as Steve finished his statement, the veterinarian entered the waiting room. He smiled. "Clover is fine. She had more of a flesh wound than anything. A little R&R and she'll be as good as new."

Willow started crying. Embry did too. "Sheesh, Mom. When you said you'd replace me I didn't think it would be with a dog." They both laughed and hugged. "Still, I'm glad you chose Clover to be my sister. I always wanted a sister."

The vet said Clover would be out of it for a while and to go ahead and go take care of police business. She would be treated as the hero she was in their absence.

Willow gave a complete accounting of everything that happened. All the evidence she'd found. And the statement by Ms. Posey, which solidified everything Willow had suspected. Ms. Posey was already at the police station telling the story in her own words by the time Steve and Willow arrived.

Ann Baker, aka Annabelle Josephine Butterfield, confessed to everything. She slipped the peanuts in her own serving bowls knowing Cookie would have those dishes washed before anything could be tested. Willow provided the perfect opportunity when she recognized Delonda and sent her soda can spinning and spraying everywhere. She tucked her peanut package in the stack of pans in the high school pantry when she slipped away to the bathroom. Then she waited for the opportune time to go back. But, by the time she went back to collect the peanut bag, Willow and her nosey daughter had found the incriminating evidence. She knew then she would have to deal with Willow. She just hadn't counted on her getting a dog. About scared her to death when she broke into the place and the dog started barking. She thought for sure she was a goner. Once she realized the dog was in a kennel, she knew she wouldn't get bit but the dog wouldn't shut up so she couldn't do what she had wanted to do...which was tear the place apart. She settled for writing a warning on her mirror and hoped that would be enough to dissuade her. She couldn't believe Willow didn't have a single tube of lipstick. She'd had to use her own, which any true southern woman would never leave home without. She hadn't realized she ripped her pants on the bush and the police found them when they searched her house.

The rest, well, Willow already figured it all out. There was no candy store to go out of business which is why there was no vlog reporting the take down. The candy store was simply Delonda's way of reminding Annabelle on an ongoing basis of the time she tried to kill Delonda. Annabelle used the story to fit in with the other suspects. Just another one of Delonda's personal vendetta take downs.

All was well at the police station and Willow just wanted to collect her dog and go home. A bath was calling her name. Willow smiled at Steve. "Can we go back to the vet's now?"

He squeezed her hand. "Yes, go. Embry, drive your mom. She gets into enough trouble navigating the streets when she isn't distracted with worry. I wouldn't want her to get into any more altercations with any rage filled drivers." He chuckled.

"Yes, sir. I will make sure she gets home."

Steve stepped close enough to Willow to kiss her. She half expected him to. Instead, he leaned down and promised he would be over later to check on her and Clover. And he would bring dinner. Maybe, just maybe, one of Oklahoma's finest hot dogs.

Embry led her mother to her car and took the keys. They had left Embry's car at the vet's and she would worry about that later. By the time they reached the vet's office, Clover was awake from her minor surgery and waiting expectantly. She had a few stitches they would have to be careful of, but, the vet allowed her to travel home with the stipulation she come back in for a checkup. Of course Willow agreed. They swung by her favorite fast food drive up and got her a cheeseburger. Willow sat in the back seat with her and fed her little bits as they drove.

Chapter 20

Willow watched Clover run through the yard. She had healed remarkably well. Willow had two storage bins of doggie treats and toys from well-wishers for a speedy recovery, especially from those who had been considered suspects. In fact, Richard had plans to open a doggie restaurant and was using Clover as his inspiration. The restaurant would carry both specialty dog dishes and people food. He had sent Clover the very first batch of specialty peanut butter treats on him. Willow shook her head from the irony. Didn't they have enough dealings with peanuts lately? Willow had no idea if people would actually frequent such a place or if the health department would allow it, but hey, he had the money to try it. Let him. She would take Clover if it ever got off the ground.

The ice cream shop was doing wonderfully. Business was booming. She had to hire a couple more employees to give her and Janie a break. And she found another lady in town to help with baking.

Molly, with the help of Beau, got her café opened in record time. Willow often had lunch with her. She loved the homemade soups Molly carried. Having Molly close by cemented the idea to add specialty coffees to her ice cream and sweet line and leave the soups and sandwiches to Molly. That worked fine with her. She even continued to sleep in. Both her new employees preferred the morning hours. Willow rarely dragged herself in before 10, and she loved it.

Summer was approaching and the city was gearing up for their ice cream festival. The whole town went crazy. There were carnival rides, ice cream eating contests, a petting zoo, all kinds of entertainment and all sorts of different foods to eat. Willow was extra excited because, being the owner of the town's one ice cream shop, she was asked to be the festival chairperson for this year's celebration. She was going to make it bigger and better than any of the previous festivals. Her only complaint was she couldn't enter the homemade ice cream contest since she was the chairwoman.

Tires crunching up the driveway distracted her from throwing the stick for Clover to fetch. She waved to Steve and he waved back.

"I see she is healing quite nicely."

Willow laughed. "Yeah, she was quite the drama queen for a little while. Talk about being a poor patient. I tried to remind her it wasn't much more than a surface wound but she wouldn't listen. Nope. In one ear and out the other. Just like my other daughter."

He grinned. "Speaking of your other daughter. Did she ever find that engagement ring?"

"Ha! No, and she just happened to end that engagement. Rather quickly I might add."

Steve took the stick from Willow and threw it out for Clover to find. "She sure is a good dog. Even if she is a bit of a drama queen."

Willow's Trophy Winning Chili

- 4lbs ground beef
- 1 lb ground pork sausage
- 1 onion, chopped
- 1 green pepper, chopped
- 1 red pepper, chopped
- 1 yellow pepper, chopped
- 18 oz tomato paste
- 1 can Progresso tomato basil soup
- 2 15 oz cans diced tomatoes, seasoned for chili
- 2 tsp hickory smoke flavored liquid smoke
- 8 Tbsp. chili powder
- 1 Tbsp. Chipotle Seasoning
- 2 Tbsp. Red Pepper Flakes
- 2 beef bouillon cubes dissolved in 2 1/2 cups water

Brown ground chuck, pork sausage, red pepper, green pepper, yellow or orange pepper, and onion in a good size Dutch oven. Add tomato paste, Progresso tomato basil soup (not the high fiber kind) del monte diced tomatoes (chili seasoned), hickory smoke flavored Liquid Smoke, Chipotle, Chili Powder, Red Pepper flakes, and the beef broth to the pot. Let simmer on low for several hours. It's best if you let the chili sit overnight, but who can wait that long? Top with chopped red onion, shredded cheddar cheese, and a dollop of sour cream.

Willow's Banana Bread

- 1 cup sugar
- 2 eggs, well beaten
- ½ c butter
- 3 tbsp. sour milk
- ½ tsp. baking soda
- 1 tsp. baking powder
- 2 c. flour
- 2 or 3 crushed ripe bananas
- 1 c. chocolate chips
- 1 c. nuts

Cream butter and sugar. Add eggs. Sift flour, baking soda, and baking powder together. Add to the wet mixture. Add remaining ingredients. Pour into well-greased loaf pan. Bake at 350 degrees for about 50 minutes or until a tooth pick tests clean. (Sour milk is prepared by adding 1 teaspoon of vinegar to milk).

Willow's Almost World Famous Cinnamon Rolls

Dough:
- 1 c. whole milk
- 3 tbsp. butter
- 3 1/2 c. all-purpose flour, divided
- 1/2 c. sugar
- 1 large egg
- 2 ¼ tsp. rapid-rise yeast (from 2 envelopes yeast)
- 1 tsp. salt
- Additional butter to grease pan

Filling:
- 3/4 c. (packed) light brown sugar
- 4 tbsp. ground cinnamon
- 1/4 c. butter, melted

Glaze:
- 8 ounces cream cheese, room temperature
- 2 c. powdered sugar
- 1/4 c. butter, room temperature

1 tsp. vanilla extract

For dough:
Combine milk and butter in glass measuring cup. Microwave on high until butter melts and mixture is slightly warm, 30 to 45 seconds. Pour into large bowl Add 1 cup flour, sugar, egg, yeast, and salt. Beat on low speed 3 minutes (with a paddle attachment if you have one), stopping occasionally to scrape down sides of bowl. Add 2 1/2 cups flour. Beat on low until flour is mixed in and dough is sticky, scraping down sides of bowl. If dough is really sticky, add more flour by tablespoonfuls until dough begins to form ball and pulls away from sides of bowl. Turn dough out onto lightly floured work surface. Knead until smooth and elastic, adding more flour if sticky, about 8 minutes. Form into ball.

Lightly oil large bowl with nonstick spray. Transfer dough to bowl, turning to coat. Cover bowl with plastic wrap, then kitchen towel. Let dough rise in a warm draft-free area until doubled in volume, about 2 hours.

For filling:

Mix brown sugar and cinnamon in medium bowl.

Punch down dough. Transfer to floured work surface. Roll out to a rectangle. Use pastry brush to apply butter to dough, leaving 1/2-inch border. Sprinkle cinnamon sugar evenly over butter. Starting at the long side, roll dough into log, pinching gently to keep it rolled up. With seam side down, cut dough crosswise with thin sharp knife into ½ inch to ¾ inch slices.

Butter two 9-inch square glass baking dishes. Divide rolls between the two baking dishes, arranging cut side up (there will be almost no space between rolls). Cover baking dishes with plastic wrap, then kitchen towel. Let dough rise in a warm draft-free area until almost doubled in size, 40 to 45 minutes.

Position rack in center of oven and preheat to 375°F. Bake rolls until tops are golden, about 20 minutes. Remove from oven and invert immediately onto rack. Cool 10 minutes. Turn rolls right side up.

For frosting:

Combine cream cheese, powdered sugar, butter, and vanilla in medium bowl. Using electric mixer, beat until smooth. Spread frosting on rolls. Serve warm or at room temperature. Goes best with a hot cup of coffee or a tall glass of milk.

Please enjoy this excerpt from 'I Scream, You Scream', Book 2 of the Willow Crier Cozy Mystery Series

Willow loved listening to the whir of her new cappuccino machine. She finally invested in re-doing the Willow Tree Sweet Shoppe and part of that renovation was a brand new specialty coffee bar. She loved the new look. She tried to please all her customers, which was tough to do since trying to please everyone has always been futile and completely against Willow's nature. Her ice cream parlor was brightly lit with colorful candy hues. The other half of her shop was now the coffee bar and it was muted and serene in earth tones. She had a glass wall built between the two dining areas to keep the coffee bar area quiet while the ice cream side was more fun and playful. While the dining area was separated, the work area behind the counter was one long service counter. Which meant any employee could take care of customers on both sides of the store. It was a big investment, but so far everyone seemed happy.

She had doubled her business since adding the coffee line. People would stop by the shop on their way to work, if they were meeting a friend, or if they just felt like a good cup of coffee to go with the book they were reading. She even had an author or two who came in regularly to write. She had no idea authors lived in her area of the world. She thought they all lived in New York or L.A. She tried to peek every now and again to see what they were working on, but she didn't want to lose their business so she tried not to be too nosy.

Today, her mystery writer was in. He pretty much kept to himself. He didn't divulge much, but once in a while he would throw out an idea and get her opinion on it. He loved her coffee and pastries. The comfortable working stations helped too.

She finished making his coffee. "Here you go, Mr. Rune." She handed him the coffee and took his fiver. They had it down to a science now. The change went into the tip jar which was split between all the employees at the end of the night.

Willow whispered his first name when he was out of range of hearing. Huxley Rune. Best-selling mystery author. New York Times Best Selling Author. She wondered if he had programmed Siri on his phone to say, "Hello New

York Times Best Selling Author" when she was addressing him. She would if she was a best-selling author.

She looked at her watch. She still had a few things to do for the ice cream festival that was kicking off the next afternoon. Including getting her shop ready for the Karaoke party which started in less than two hours.

Mr. Rune would be taking his computer and leaving for the night when he realized what would be going on. Karaoke. The town loved it. He hated it.

Her glass partition wall was on a track and could be opened to make one big room for bigger parties. She loved it. She had so many options with this new system.

The guy she hired to run the karaoke walked through the door and she waved him over. She had a little stage in the coffee shop side, which she used for open mic night as well as karaoke.

"Hey, Mitch, what would you like to drink?"

He perused the menu. "Hmm, how about a bigger Frappuccino?"

"Okay, I'll get it ready for you." She had gone with big, bigger, and biggest to describe her drink sizes for the 12, 16, and 20 ounce size cups.

She enjoyed being different. It was what set her apart.

As she was making the drink, she noticed Clyde come in. Clyde was fairly rotund with thinning hair and few teeth shy of a mouthful. He clearly was missing a few in the brains department as well. Some said he was just a little slow because he took drugs when he was younger while others said he was disabled. Willow wasn't sure which it was, but when he was around trouble usually followed close behind. And since her days as a murder suspect a few weeks before, Willow was trying to keep her nose clean. Which was, for some reason, really hard to do. Because trouble also liked to follow her around. Put her and Clyde in the same room together and trouble pretty much was a guarantee.

She watched him carefully.

He walked straight to Mr. Rune's table and started speaking and gesturing with his hands. The way he talked, in a kind of a slow whine, made it difficult for Willow to hear.

The blender mixing the frap didn't help her hearing abilities either. She turned the blender off and filled the glass, topped it off with whipped cream, and a drizzle of chocolate and caramel, stuck a straw in it then took it to Mitch who was already setting up. She couldn't help it if Mr. Rune's table was near the stage, could she?

She had no idea Clyde knew Mr. Rune. None whatsoever. She was close enough to hear the words "money, cheated, never again," and "you'll pay." Hmm…wonder what happened between the two of them?

Clyde left right after speaking with the author. Mr. Rune went back to his writing like nothing had happened. Maybe this time she was wrong. Maybe Clyde hadn't brought trouble with him.

Mitch finished setting up and a few minutes later Mr. Rune ordered another coffee, although this time, it was to go. He knew it was about to get loud and, well, loud wasn't the writer's style. He gathered up his belongings and put them in his leather brief case then took his coffee and left. She wouldn't see him until after the ice cream festival. She had tried to talk him into participating but he muttered something about deadlines, rewrites, and time, then shook his head and stalked off, obviously in a mood. She had thought perhaps having a famous writer's name attached to the ice cream festival would bring in some much needed income for the town.

The other writer in town, Jasper Cliffhanger, volunteered to help. Willow was glad for the help, but, because the writer wasn't well known he wasn't going to attract a crowd like Huxley Rune would have. Oh well, you can't have it all.

6:30. 30 minutes until show time. She opened the glass partition and one of her part timers helped her rearrange the tables and chairs, making sure there was plenty of room for all who wanted to attend.

Willow was surprised to see Clyde return. He ordered a chocolate milk shake, found a table, and waited for the fun to begin.

Karaoke was in full swing. Willow had brought in two of her part timers and Janie, her best friend, who normally worked the morning shift to help with the crowd. Business was booming. She finally felt like she was starting to become part of the town. Last month's fiasco with the chili cook-off almost sent her packing.

She smiled as three teen age girls took the stage. The music started up and all three of them were giggling. As the music they chose filled the room, Clyde flew up out of his chair in a rage. He took long strides and approached the stage. He was shaking his head and telling them he didn't like the song they were singing. This time Willow got involved.

"Clyde, leave the girls alone."

"This isn't an appropriate song. They have to stop singing this song."

Willow recognized the song as an upbeat song sung by the Dixie Chicks. Apparently some people still harbored bitterness over the chicks' political position they took years ago. "Clyde, the girls aren't making a political statement. They are just singing a fun song about a guy named Earl. Leave them alone."

He walked back to his table, complaining as he went. "They shouldn't sing this song. It's not right. This is an American celebration."

Willow understood. Back in the day she hadn't been pleased about the route the singing group took in expressing their opinions either. In fact, she threw away the cds she owned of theirs. But, years had passed and she'd learned you have to forgive and move on or the bitterness would eat you up. Besides, the Earl song was fun. It even made her smile.

As soon as she was behind the counter, the loud pounding music came to an abrupt halt. The entire system had stopped working. She scanned the room and found Clyde on his hands and knees by the electrical outlet. She blew out an aggravated breath then confronted Clyde.

"Clyde, you are done here. You are not welcome in my shop. You are banned."

He started to protest. "That is a bad song. You shouldn't let them sing that song. Earl Rune had to die. It's a bad song."

Willow thought she heard him wrong. "Clyde, did you say the song is about Earl Rune? Mr. Rune's first name is Huxley, not Earl. Okay? The song isn't about Mr. Rune. The song is just pretend. Someone made it up. It's not about anyone in particular." She paused to see if he was listening to her. "You need to go home, Clyde. We'll talk tomorrow to see if you are banned. I don't want to ban you but you can't be doing things like that. It isn't polite."

"Earl Rune had to die. Earl Rune had to die." He muttered as he left the coffee shop.

Author Bio

Lilly York? (aka Darlene Shortridge, author of Contemporary Christian Fiction) How about Lilly Belle; a mis-plant northerner, living in a southern world. Southern charm is lost among late nights with a two year old granddaughter, heat flashes competing with hell, copious re-runs of Murder She Wrote with Jessica Fletcher catching the bad guy, and a vivid imagination keeping insanity at bay.

In both humor and mystery, Lilly draws inspiration from terrible twos, a 24 year old daughter who questions her sanity, a son who constantly spews bad puns, and a husband who has selective hearing. Though, that's perfectly alright with her, because what can you love more than a good laugh and a family so dysfunctional they almost seem functional?

To stay informed on the whereabouts and goings-on of the Willow Crier Cozy Mystery Characters as well as upcoming releases, recipes and maybe a clue or two, join Lilly's e-mail club by going to…

LillyYork.com

,0086

Made in the USA
Lexington, KY
14 October 2017